About the Author

Jonathan Stanyer is an English teacher, having taught extensively in the UK as well as abroad, including Chieti, Italy, where the ideas for Italian crime stories first germinated in his mind! He is married with one child and currently divides his time between Milton Keynes, Istanbul and the Middle East.

Blessed Spirits

Jonathan Stanyer

Blessed Spirits

Olympia Publishers
London

www.olympiapublishers.com
OLYMPIA PAPERBACK EDITION

A CIP catalogue record for this title is
available from the British Library.

ISBN: 978-1-80439-278-2

This is a work of fiction.
Names, characters, places and incidents originate from the writer's
imagination. Any resemblance to actual persons, living or dead, is
purely coincidental.

First Published in 2024

Olympia Publishers
Tallis House
2 Tallis Street
London
EC4Y 0AB

Printed in Great Britain

Dedication

Dedicated to my late English teacher at Bedford Modern School, Barry Stafford. He showed me how to use words and appreciate their power. To him, my grateful thanks.

List of Characters

Captain Arthur Edwards, British army Major
Major Aldo Molina – fascist officer
Margarette Embriaco – anti fascist soldier
Testaladi Maglio – anti fascist soldier
Present day
Ronnie Cabot – English teacher
Darius Celestini – English language school owner, Ronnie's employer
Inspector Giordano Bruno – Head of Abruzzo Maritime Criminal Investigation Unit
Detective Sergeant Amanda 'Mandy' Chilabon – AMCIU
Inspector Domenico Drago – Head of Rome Criminal Investigation Unit
Anna Bianchi – university student
Tomaso Scilaci – caretaker, uncle of the above
Paolo Pescalodi – plumber employed by Darius Celestini
Patricia Ener – newly qualified Forensic Pathologist
Bernadette Kenny – English teacher
Orazio Mancetti – Christian Liberal Party Secretary Chieti [1] branch
Mauro Andretti – local English student
Danielle Entrada – local English student
Simone Ribetti – barman at CLP headquarters
Tiziana Sangregorio – secretary at Chieti branch of language school

---

[1] 'Chieti' is pronounced 'Key – a – tea'

Contessa D'Lanciano – Ronnie's neighbour
Bernardo d'Avenzano – Chieti Scalo railway station manager: English student
Station Sergeant Filipo Degrelli – Police officer
Constable Castello – Police officer
Ella Frantoni – employee at Chieti Comune : Bruno's girlfriend
Violetta Crimosa – cleaner employed by Darius celestini
Michele Ceresa – secretary at Chieti Comune
Constable Carboni – Police officer
Constable Prestimone – Police officer
Gianni Tedescho – Chieti jeweller, local English student
Iani Stanieri – taxi driver
Innocent Lollis – lawyer
Cesare Frantoni – Pescara architect – Ella's brother
old Vasco (+son) – farmhouse residents on Darius' property
Deputy Director General Cosimo Nerone – top regional policeman
Giacomo Lettieri – National Secretary CLP
Constable Vivante – Police officer
Signor Gallorio – head of foreign language department, Pescara University
Vincente Mancetti – brother of Orazio

Prologue

August 1944 – Francavilla al Mare, Abruzzo; the German retreat from central Italy.

The captured Italian fascist officer dressed in his dusty black uniform was roughly sat in the back of the British army jeep by two determined, battle-weary British commandos, weary from the recent gun battle that killed or captured most of his comrades, some of whom lay dead on the verges all around them.

This black shirt officer sat dishevelled and defiant – a pair of angry dark eyes glared out from underneath a tattered officer's black cap, hands tied to metal panels either side of him by thin hemp. It was the best the army could find in the circumstances.

'You two, over here!' Captain Arthur Edwards shouted, pointing to two militia fighters, whose fighting unit had captured the black shirt officer. Edwards walked up to the jeep, brushing down the dust and dirt on his uniform and put his cap on straight. Captain Edwards thought for a second before turning to address the large group of anti-fascist militia, sitting down along roadside grass verges, resting from the recent battle. British, Canadian and the aforesaid anti-fascist fighters had all fought hand-to-hand as they had helped liberate local pro-German fascist headquarters in Francavilla, on the Adriatic coast of central Italy. 'My unit,' he said indicating with his swagger stick those nearest him, 'has been given orders to support the drive on Pescara.' Behind him the straggling column of light tanks, lorries and jeeps were starting their engines and moving off, churning up giant clouds of summer dust.

11

Not asking if the two Italian anti-fascist volunteers he had picked out from a group near him could either understand him or even drive a jeep, Edwards continued. '...so, I need two volunteers to drive *him*,' indicating the captured officer, 'over to regimental headquarters in, and looking on the map spread on a neighbouring jeep with two sergeants, "Sulmona, okay?"'

'Si,' the heavily armed female fighter replied languidly, putting out her cigarette, picking up her sub machine gun and taking the keys from Captain Edwards' open hand. Her male companion, equally heavily armed with a bazooka languidly nodded as he loitered by the Jeep's bonnet. Behind the two fighters several of their comrades made gestures of tightening a noose round a neck with abject glee towards the dejected albeit defiant captive. Cursory salutes were exchanged as the two fighters got into the jeep after jeering at their prisoner who sat sullenly in the back. If Edwards were honest, he was glad to get the captured fascist officer off his hands and let the local militia deal with him. It wasn't unheard of however, for anti-fascists to summarily execute captured fascists with or without allied permission but he didn't have time to dwell on morality.

'Sir?' Edwards' Adjutant put down his radio headphones and ran over as the jeep set off down the slope towards the valley bottom via a winding road. 'He wasn't searched properly, the prisoner I mean.'

'What?' Edwards sighed as he surveyed the smoke from the burning palazzo complex swirled all around him resulting from the gun battle that had raged throughout what had until this afternoon been the local fascist militia's headquarters. 'It's too late for that now,' he replied, his eyes looking north west where his unit was urgently needed in the drive to clear Abruzzo of Germans. 'Just organise a detail to clear the bodies off the road so we can get going!'

Present Day

Thursday 26 January – Seven Thirty p.m.

In order to examine the decayed broken boiler, Signor Paolo Pescalodi, the somewhat decayed, Shakespearean looking plumber had had to force open the old heavy wooden door that allowed access.

Then, shining his torch into the gloomy ground floor cubbyhole, he could see a faded white wrought iron container sitting on a square of bricks attached to the floor; tatty old pipes and cobwebs protruding from all sides with God knows what wildlife lurking in the shadows. No one had examined *this* boiler for decades probably – and given its condition, Pescalodi didn't fancy being the first either!

The man whose apartment the boiler had provided hot water for, an Englishman named Ronnie Cabot, stood a few feet away in his winter greatcoat and boots, nervously watching the inviting prospect of a hot bath that evening, disappear down the proverbial plug-hole. His top floor rent-free apartment had been provided by his employer, Darius Celestini who owned a string of English language study schools in the local area – Ronnie taught English in the Chieti Scalo branch, a few miles away down the valley towards the regional hub, Pescara situated on the Adriatic Sea.

Muttering away to himself, Pescalodi next prodded away the rotten panelling with the handle end of his screwdriver and batted down cobwebs from around the boiler like a demented orchestral conductor. Then, kicking at what he thought was a decayed piece of skirting board his boot encountered something hard. Taking out a small silver-coloured torch, he shone it on what seemed like an old shop dummy covered in hardened sediment and dust. Hesitatingly, in case something bit him maybe, he reached out, trying to work out what the obstruction was.

Letting out a 'Va fangulo!' as if he had been bitten, he dropped whatever it was and taking a noisy dusty step back, trod on Ronnie's right foot.

'Fuck! Watch out you old git! Cabot shouted.

Pescalodi, not familiar with English slang, recovered his balance, shrugged and carried on his inspection regardless.

Cabot and Pescalodi's eyes were then riveted on the plumber's right hand as he reached it back into the space behind the boiler, picking up an unmistakable object.

A mummified human arm.

An arm that had, on closer inspection, been connected to a mummified body covered in dirty dusty rags and shreds of rotten plasterboard.

Expressions of shock and anger resonated throughout the rest of the palazzo as the elderly plumber then performed a little impromptu dance holding the remains of a body as if it had been glued to him.

Finally he sat down shocked on the concrete floor opposite and collected his thoughts.

Ronnie, equally grubby now and speechless, sat opposite him.

A pause while both parties took in what they had found before Ronnie told Paolo in basic Italian to call the police.

*

And so, while living and working in the picturesque and ancient hill town of Chieti in central Italy, the said Ronnie Cabot, a mid-twenties English teacher and avid amateur historian from Yorkshire, became involved in a strange series of events that had begun in the basement of his residence.

His apartment, being situated in one corner of an enormous square 19th century Baroque complex of decorous, high ceilinged albeit draughty apartments, went by the grand name of *Palazzo Gran Sasso.* The enormous brooding edifice overlooked Chieti's main street, the Corso Marrucino.

Access to his top floor flat was via a series of imposing marble staircases with extravagantly sculptured turn of the century mouldings and fittings.

Extensive dark blue carpeting covered the central strip of light blue marble palazzo corridor floors, which being open to the elements on one side explained its faded, weather-beaten appearance.

The rickety rackety boiler that heated Ronnie's apartment had first become an issue once the temperature started to drop at the onset of winter. The loud wheezing and gurgling of the pipes in his apartment made it obvious it wasn't going to see out another campaign.

Ronnie's Italian though, hadn't stretched as far as complaining to the palazzo's caretaker, a laconic man somewhere around late middle-age, always to be seen with a grubby grey raincoat and flat grey cap. Allegedly in charge of the whole palazzo's maintenance, he was mainly to be seen opening and closing the barrier in front of the palazzo to allow residents in their cars to access secure car parking, receiving tips for finding

15

the best spots. According to Signor Darius Celestini, Ronnie's employer, the caretaker was also a mine of information on the comings and goings of those who lived in the building information he occasionally shared with the local police force. Like him, loathe him or supremely indifferent, the residents especially those with cars, couldn't really avoid him if they wanted to park securely so they tended to deal with him with fixed smiles, keeping him sweet with generous tips at Easter and Christmas.

Upon hearing Ronnie's mangled Italian complaints about the draughty apartment, the caretaker shrugged his chunky shoulders and walked off, perhaps not caring too much about an old corpse or trying to make sense of the foreigner's bad Italian, abruptly retreating into his comfy sentry box in front of the palazzo's grandiose *fin-de-siecle* entrance, heated with an electric fire and closing the door.

'Well, fuck you,' Cabot considered, deciding to leave the caretaker's uninterested behaviour for now as he had set off to work a few days previously Though Cabot had then purchased an electric bar-fire, hiss increasing frustration at living in a draughty apartment had now reached its limit. Darius had originally put him in the spacious apartment when it was warm and sunny outside but now it was winter, the apartment needed heating properly. The caretaker now having gone off duty, Cabot had then decided to drag his employer away from *his* comfy home and do something about Cabot's cold home – that evening!

*

Ronnie had read in a guidebook to Italy before arriving in the country that said, in a solemn tone, that Italians regarded dinner time as an almost religious experience and would not allow themselves to be interrupted in its celebration. Being an Englishman, brought up in the "eat it while it's hot," ideology, he had no such qualms interrupting Darius while he was at home attending culinary communion at dinner; indeed Ronnie's pissed off tone was sufficient for his employer to not bother telling him off for phoning him out of hours. Darius immediately sent round his in-house plumber, the aged Signor Pescalodi to try and resuscitate his English teacher's dilapidated central heating system.

The semi-retired workman, wearing a large red baseball hat and not unlike an unkempt version of Super Mario, seemed quite jovial considering the freezing weather and the latish hour; probably on double time, Ronnie considered.

Ronnie had hoped so.

Darius could afford it after all. Paolo as it happened, worked for him, mostly anyway and as he generally did a good job, was kept on a retainer, it later transpired.

A quirk of construction meant Ronnie's hot water tank was on the ground floor of the palazzo so hot water was pumped *up* to his apartment on the fifth floor.

*

Ronnie's watch crept towards eleven p.m.

Several Italian *Carabinieri* (along with an ambulance crew) had by now arrived and were guarding a cordoned-off area around the site of the boiler. A white suited forensics' unit bathed in a strong arc-light photographed the mummified corpse as well as the location it had been found in… The ambulance crew was then allowed to transport the body away on a stretcher with a pathologist in attendance to monitor the proceedings.

Darius, having arrived after Ronnie's frantic phone call,

stood with him outside the cordon attempting every so often to question the police officers as events unfolded. He hadn't learnt much, though it was *his* boiler and indeed *his* property everyone and his dog was poking over now. A Carabinieri officer told him to contact the police headquarters in the morning.

Pescalodi, the plumber now stood fidgeting nearby, probably waiting for Darius to pay him and let him finally go home.

A forensics technician dressed in a protective white suit covering her head except for gauze patches over her mouth and eyes was carefully examining the hole where the body had been, made easier now since the rusting wrought iron boiler had also been removed. Using tweezers she carefully collected fibres strewn on the chalky dusty floor before putting them in a tamper evidence bag. She then carefully held, in two forensically-gloved fingers, an old leather belt with faded lettering that couldn't be read except for 'Italia' which could still be made out etched into it.

This particular find seemed to galvanise the anxious hovering Darius even at this late hour in his huddled brown raincoat. A long monologue in the local Chieti dialect ensued with the forensic technician while she had been trying to do her job of recording everything found. Being interrupted in increasing degrees of anger by this annoying man dancing around her like a pesky fly was not conducive to carrying out a sensitive investigation. Indeed, she had been about to ask one of the policeman to remove the annoying man when a metallic ocean blue Alfa Romeo police car then pulled up quietly at the entrance to the palazzo complex, temporarily blocking several parked cars.

The driver's door opened and a tall man in his fifties dressed in a dark suit and grey raincoat got out.

Striding purposely up to the site of the grim discovery, he flashed his ID card and received the salutes of the two Carabinieri officers guarding the cordoned-off basement area.

The forensic pathologist, seeing the new arrival, stood up, took off a latex white glove and shook hands with the man obviously in charge hereabouts of investigating criminality at all times of the day and night.

'Inspector Giordano Bruno, Head of Abruzzo Maritime Criminal Investigation Unit,' he said introducing himself to the forensics pathologist with a concurrent easy smile trying to and mostly succeeding in shielding his surprise at meeting a female forensic pathologist in the world of investigating violent deaths.

This man had the air of a surgeon, those who knew him considered, rather than a policeman.

Long fingers with manicured nails that could easily apply stitches as much as handcuffs.

Inspector Bruno in response would say he *was* a kind of surgeon except he operated on diseases that latched themselves onto civilised society.

'Ten words to introduce yourself inspector!' the female replied without looking up while holding faded linen fibres in a set of tweezers under a magnifying glass.

'Why did you remove the body before I had arrived?' Bruno replied, ignoring the pathologist's attempt at humour.

'I decided it was appropriate!' she replied.

'Who gave you permission?' the inspector asked, sounding out the still unintroduced female pathologist who stood like a sentinel guarding her territory.

'See that cordon Giordano? Inside that area is *my* space,' she added with a wry smile and a furrowed brow. 'Outside *there,* that's your world,' she indicated with a forensic gloved index finger.

Inspector Bruno inwardly reeling from being spoken to like

a naughty schoolboy with his first name indeed followed her pointing finger into the middle distance.

'Patricia Ener, just graduated from the oldest forensic medicine school in Italy in Turin,' she smiled, turning to face him, latex gloved hands on hips. 'This is my first case!'

Inspector Bruno, intrigued by the woman's natural air of authority and deciding he needed no further explanation of his and her limits of authority, peered at a collection of bandages Ener was now brandishing under his nose. The last thing he needed was to sneeze and show himself up so continued to listen attentively.

'I found a lot of these wrapped up withy the body, inspector, so they should help me get an idea how long the body's been here?'

Constrained by the police cordon tape, Inspector Bruno nodded sagely before stepping back to consider his next move.

A few lace curtains fluttered around the grand palazzo apartment windows as anxious twitchers heard the inspector's initial foray and the pathologist's slight put down. This was better than what was on Rai Uno TV.

Bruno, eager to show he was as capable of thinking on his feet hit back. 'If you had said Pathologist five times, you would be as important as me then signora! Please call me, Jordi. I am just a cop who wants to solve cases and please my myself, my boss and my conscience, probably in that order!'

'I hope I will be able to help you then!' Ener added as she turned to go back to work.

'You haven't worked with a female forensic pathologist before then inspector?' Ener asked while on her knees sifting dust from the concrete floor.

'We are not *that* entirely backward here in the provinces

signora,' Bruno replied, smiling. 'My very capable detective sergeant is female. It is the quality of your work I am interested in, not your gender!'

'Aha!' Ener smiled. 'Well, I might say straight away that this corpse has been here *a long time*.'

Bruno peered in, forced to agree with her initial pronouncement. 'Which is older then, signora? The boiler or *it* ?'

'My autopsy report will be with you as soon as possible,' Ener replied without looking at Bruno while on her knees in front of the body, directing the forensic photographer to record every angle of the location.

The inspector had seen enough and left the pathologist to it.

*

Ronnie, standing on the edge of the little group of concerned residents following events couldn't get any of the animated conversation between Inspector Bruno and Pathologist Ener going on a few metres away.

He then decided without ceremony and having given up on getting any hot water, to return to his cold apartment, his mind turning over the night's strange discovery.

'The police will visit your apartment tomorrow, okay?' Darius shouted in English after consulting with Inspector Bruno, seeing Ronnie near the top of the first set of marble stairs. Cabot put out a thumbs up, continuing to climb without turning round.

'Wait a minute please, Ronnie,' Darius then shouted after a few seconds before sprinting away into the darkness.

Ronnie turned, stood and waited on the penultimate step before a wide marble landing.

Presently, Darius returned with a new fan heater still in its

21

box under his arm. Walking up to Ronnie and smiling, he handed it over, not knowing Ronnie had already purchased one, but a nice gesture all the same. Darius was paying his teacher's utility bills anyway so would have a nice surprise when he received the next bi-monthly one.

'Thanks,' Ronnie replied, half-smiling turning and trudging back upstairs leaving the group below to disperse when they were done. He realised he almost liked his invariably snappily dressed middle aged employer who had described himself down the phone to Ronnie in the UK as a "local businessman," which involved amongst other activities, owning and running an English language school in the locality. It was particularly apt, Ronnie thought, when Darius told him his family also exported olive oil as he was then currently reading *"The Godfather,"* wherein, the gangster Corleone family were also colourfully (self-)described as olive oil exporters. Darius even gave him a bottle of his family's olive oil as a house-warming present when Cabot moved into the apartment provided by Darius upon arrival in Chieti.

Was Darius "connected" too?

A smile played on Ronnie's face as he mused the implications, though as events subsequently transpired, it turned out to be not such a fanciful proposition.

Friday 27 January – 7.20 a.m.

The denizens of the slumbering ancient hill town of Chieti awoke under a grey fog bank of mist.

On a good day, the inhabitants of the baroque mansions as well as newer apartment blocks that flanked either side of the long rectangular ridge the town was situated on, could indeed call themselves kings of the world.

This was why the Romans had fortified the site two thousand years ago.

Views north and south across rolling valleys were unbroken as far as the eye could see.

Looking east if you were able to, and the blues and greens of the Adriatic sea were spread out along the coast contrasting with the brighter shades of blue above.

If it weren't for the small matter of the imposing Apennine mountains to the west, Chieti's residents could probably kid themselves they could see Rome herself on a good day.

Ronnie's room faced west.

Beyond the huddle of dark reds and greys of the roofs on the other side of the narrow street opposite Ronnie's building, the snow-clad mountains stood sentinel, as they had for untold millennia until a motorway and railway had forced their way through in more recent times.

That morning heavy snow was heading Chieti's way.

Ronnie and his fellow *Chietinos* had been warned.

With the electric fire on in his kitchen while Ronnie made

breakfast, at least one room of his draughty lodgings was warm enough to sit in.

Outside, with the temperature hovering around zero, occasional street sounds of people and cars drifted up from below. As he usually didn't start teaching until the afternoon, he could take things slowly, albeit with several Italian detectives creeping around his flat at some point during the day as Darius then had called to inform him. Indeed, because of the search of Ronnie's apartment in connection with the grim discovery downstairs, Darius said he would give Ronnie the day off – with pay!

'I want you there when they search,' he said.

'Why?' Ronnie asked.

'In case they find anything,' came the enigmatic reply.

'Like what?'

Darius didn't answer.

Ronnie tried a new tack.

'What about a new boiler?' he asked.

'I will send Signor Pescalodi to install a new one today.'

'Today?' This sounded too good to be true.

Having lived in the apartment for about four months, it seemed to him unlikely there was anything of interest to the police there; the mystery of the disappearing heat had been solved downstairs surely, he thought as he went to look out of his living-room window to the street below. Ronnie could just see the caretaker's legs as he sat in his small square black booth heated by his electric fire. Normally a strident little man who paced the boundaries of his palazzo empire on a daily basis like a soldier on sentry duty. Today however, he wasn't pacing around; his sentry box window was also closed.

Probably the inclement weather, Ronnie thought.

*

Eleven a.m.

Ronnie had been indeed waiting, reading at his small kitchen table for the policeman who duly introduced himself as Inspector Giordano Bruno upon arrival at Ronnie's front door.

An equally statuesque female dressed in a business suit and carrying an iPad along with a fair-sized handbag followed him in.

'This is my colleague Signor Cabot,' Bruno introduced his assistant. 'Detective Sergeant Amanda Chilabon,' he added as Cabot went to shake hands.

Introductions were conducted, Cabot reflected, with a woman with smallish fingers for a tall person.

He decided not to mention his reflection to her.

'Your name sounds like *chilly bones*,' Ronnie hazarded with a smile, trying to make polite conversation.

'Aaah!' Amanda's English realised this was an attempt at English humour. She decided to throw him a lifeline as the officers around her started their search. 'My parents loved "Winnie the Pooh" books so they named me after one of the poems,' she told the English teacher, putting her notepad down. 'Chilabon means happy house in our old dialect,' she added.

'What is the matter with Amanda Jane…?' Ronnie reeled off, hoping the policewoman would get the joke.

DS Chilabon did indeed smile at Cabot's ready production of her favourite poem.

'I didn't know Pooh books were read in Italy,' Cabot continued, taken off-guard by a conversation about English poetry by an attractive woman in his own apartment. He couldn't help but be intrigued by her particularly as she seemed about his own age and only a centimetre or so taller.

25

'Well, there it is,' she continued as she seemed to read his mind. 'The collected poems of AA Milne are pride of place on my bookshelf!' she added with a chuckle while simultaneously carrying on a dialogue with the accompanying police officers and making notes on her iPad.

Inspector Bruno gravitated towards the easy chat between the apartment occupant and his DS though obviously not on the grave matter in hand.

Bruno wasn't as up to date on literary analysis as Chilabon and Cabot so with a motion of his head Bruno directed Chilabon to assist the search.

Cabot then slunk back to the kitchen to await the result of the police search, unable though to repress a little smile at the easy connection he had made with the pretty upholder of the law.

*

The policemen searching the cupboards, floors and even the ceiling were quiet but diligent while Inspector Bruno moved from room to room to oversee their work. Notes were made with several photos taken on police iPads.

'Sorry, I couldn't introduce myself last night Signor Cabot,' Bruno put his head round the kitchen door apologising to the Englishman and putting him at his ease. 'Very distressing for you, I'm sure the discovery in your old boiler room downstairs,' he continued. 'But I am sure that the mystery can be solved.'

Here was a seasoned policeman, Ronnie considered, who couldn't help but radiate a calm confident air, a special skill in the chaos of a crime scene such as the one Ronnie and the policeman had encountered the previous night.

'Thank you inspector,' Cabot smiled as they shook hands. 'I just hope Signor Celestini can get this mystery sorted and my apartment can be warm again.'

'Of course,' Bruno replied – his alert eyes were already looking past the Englishman, taking in everything around him in the whitewashed sparsely furnished apartment.

Jordi Bruno's swept back black hair reminded Cabot of a younger version of Christopher Lee. Cabot however, decided not to mention the policeman's likeness to Dracula as an opening gambit if he wanted to get on Chieti's top policeman's better side. (Cabot was still technically an illegal worker as Darius Celestini still hadn't sorted out Ronnie's residence permit, despite Ronnie pestering him to do so).

Ronnie wouldn't mind being questioned by DS Chilabon again though – in a comfortable wine bar, preferably.

The CIU chief also spoke excellent English.

Not, Ronnie thought, got from a provincial language school as Bruno continued to question Ronnie: How long he had lived in the apartment?

Any other problems he had noticed in the property?

Inspector Giordano Bruno, in quiet moments of introspection considered himself well-spoken – a polymath indeed, as well as being a successful state sponsored thief-taker. His devout Catholic parents had named him ironically after a 16th century monk, considered a heretic by the Catholic Inquisition of the time for daring to propagate the idea the God had created other life in the universe apart from on Earth.

Jordi Bruno hadn't considered himself currently in the Holy Office's gunsights, though he reckoned there were plenty of faces he had put away over the years who would happily pay for a prime spot to watch him toast nicely in a nearby public square. Bruno was only interested in gazing into people's souls if criminality was lurking therein, regardless of who they were.

Which God they prayed to, if any, was irrelevant to him.

27

Ronnie Cabot's eyes enviously sized up Inspector Bruno's designer sunglasses after the inspector had taken them off, folded carefully and put into his jacket pocket after a little excursion onto the balcony.

Looking for any clues lurking there, Cabot wondered?

A bit of a fashion diva when he could afford to be, Ronnie Cabot instantly wished *he* possessed such a pair – unlikely presently on an English teacher's modest salary in those parts but not out of reach.

While Ronnie stood envying the fashionable eyewear, the inspector, oblivious of Ronnie's beady eyes, was making extensive notes on his iPad. Pertinent to the sombre matter in hand, Jordi Bruno then matter-of-factly informed Cabot as they sat in the bright living room later that the body found in the basement seemed to be a soldier, probably from the style of uniform, fighting on the allied side in the last war.

Cabot didn't really know what to think at this point but just listen as Bruno continued in flawless English.

In late 1944, the Chieti area was liberated by British and Canadian forces, the inspector informed him. German forces, he continued, then retreated further north to Pescara, the regional coastal centre where their resistance would prove more protracted. Local German collaborators had, however, fought on around Chieti, knowing what would happen to them if they were captured by anti-fascist Italian militiamen fighting with the allies. Ronnie's top floor apartment, Bruno told him had been notorious during the German occupation.

'Why?' Ronnie asked.

'Your balcony was where the chief fascist collaborator used to sit and watch over the main street, often holding a hunting rifle,' Bruno replied, walking over to Ronnie's balcony and throwing open its doors for the second time. A cold wind was briefly given the freedom of the whole apartment.

'God! Really?' Ronnie let out with some surprise. 'Is there a connection between my apartment and what you found last night then?'

'There may well be,' Bruno replied. 'The water pipes are yours certainly signor. I shall hopefully get some more details as soon as the pathologist tells me,' he said smiling and getting to his feet. Then, calling the assembled police searchers into Ronnie's hallway for a quick evaluation on what had been discovered, if anything, he spoke again smiling to the tenant. 'I may need to speak to you again Signor Cabot about the apartment but next I shall interview those connected to the property such as your employer at the police station to see if they can shed light on the affair.'

What Inspector Bruno had to smile about was a mystery.

He didn't have to live in such a notorious apartment.

The cops had spent nearly an hour prodding skirting boards, floorboards and looking behind several large items of furniture Ronnie had inherited when Darius had moved him in.

Apart from the two uniformed Carabinieri policemen, Bruno seemed to have bought his well-tailored suits from where Darius evidently got his.

The search finally over, the law along with DS Chilabon soon politely departed though not before Inspector Bruno and Ronnie swapped mobile phone numbers.

Cabot was then left to wonder the next step.

The top floor apartment had seemed innocuous enough when Ronnie had moved in, though the whole place had obviously been deep cleaned as there was the lingering smell of fresh paint and disinfectant.

Had Inspector Bruno picked up on that?

Ronnie's apartment did enjoy good views from the front balcony, as Bruno had pointed out. The central Italian Apennine mountains and the highest mountain in particular, *Gran Sasso,* after which his building was named were particularly visible, on a good day anyway. Cabot could also watch the goings-on of a good chunk of the main Corso as it wended its way through Chieti. However, the palazzo's access corridors on the opposite side of his apartment were open to the sky on one side and a car park below. He tried to imagine a swaggering wartime fascist sitting on his balcony armed with a rifle with telescopic sights and threatening the locals going about their business below in the way he had seen the Ralph Fiennes' character conduct himself in *Schindler's List.*

Ronnie Cabot too was usually armed on the balcony, on sunny days anyway, with nothing more sinister than an English newspaper and a cold beer. *He* couldn't threaten anyone in the street unless he played his music too loudly on his balcony or made paper darts to throw onto the heads of unsuspecting passers-by far below!

During the day, cars and buses snaked their way along the Corso avoiding pedestrians trying to get across the road. In the evenings however, vehicles were banned as pedestrians took their traditional evening strolls. Always dressed in best clothes meeting and greeting the same people they saw every day, the local population engaged in a sort of prelapsarian ceremony of peace and goodwill to all men and women encountered along the Corso.

If Ronnie had a decent suit and was armed with the inspector's designer sunglasses, he would amble along the Corso, preferably with a nice girl on his arm, greeting the great and the good like a film star acknowledging the cheers of his fans. (Better not share that analogy with his many students – they wouldn't thank him for being lumped into the category of his adoring admirers).

Anyway, compared to Milton Keynes where he lived in the UK, Chieti did seem to Ronnie on occasion, like one big family especially when everyone was outside and socialising of an evening.

*

Five p.m.

Walking to the tram stop across the little Gran Sasso square, having bought the requisite tickets from genial Enrico who sold them from his little Tobacconist's shop, Ronnie got a call from Darius. Had the police found anything he was keen to find out?

Ronnie replied in the negative, as far as he knew. Ronnie was then to leave his key under his doormat if he went out so Paolo Pescalodi the plumber could access his flat to install new pipes for the new digital boiler downstairs where the crime scene had recently wrapped up. As Ronnie was already outside and heading for his tram stop to go to work, he had to quickly pop back upstairs to leave the key under his doormat as Darius had asked him to.

Returning downstairs to the main street, Ronnie stopped in his tracks.

He felt the distinct sensation of a cold spot blocking his way on the last set of stairs to reach the ground floor.

31

He also realised that even the breezes that blew and eddied around the staircases and residents, up to his very front door sometimes, had been unable to shift it after vaguely noticing its recent appearance.

He couldn't avoid this mass of cold so had to briskly walk through it like everyone else descending from upstairs apartments.

Other residents must have noticed it too, he thought later that afternoon returning from work.

He mentioned it in his basic Italian, to the beyond-retirement-age woman who 'cleaned' the turn of the century corridors and stairs most days during the week.

He received a sinister response.

'Your fault,' she said emphatically in Italian, slow enough even for Ronnie to understand.

She pointed at him with a bony finger, 'You released her, so she sits there,' the old lady continued haranguing at him while leaning on the corridor balustrade, smoking a smelly Italian cigarette on one of her numerous "breaks."

'Me? Her?' Ronnie responded in some surprise, taken slightly aback. 'What are you talking about?' He asked. 'Why me…?'

'She now wants justice,' she said interrupting him in her crackly Italian, with a faraway look in her eyes before putting her fag butt into a small box she carried in her pocket, picking up her plastic bucket and heading off down the corridor.

She looked so frail Ronnie thought she was more likely to fall *in* the bucket than clean anything with it.

*

'Tell me about the palazzo. You do maintenance for Signor Celestini?' Inspector Bruno was leaning over the elderly plumber, his tall stature fishing for anything that might help the inspector after requesting the elderly man to come to the police station for an interview.

He wasn't catching much.

'I maintain it inspector, I don't go digging in it,' Pescalodi whined, looking up Bruno's nose. 'Signor Celestini pays me for any little plumbing or electrical jobs that's all,' he said with both hands open palms upwards as if records of his good deeds were therein inscribed.

'Have you ever seen anything suspicious during your work at the palazzo?'

Pescalodi paused visibly, eyes scanning the interview room for a hidden altercation if he stepped out of line.

Inspector Bruno took the pause as a suspicious action so moved his face within six inches of the gnarled anxious features of Signor Pescalodi.

'If I find out you're holding out on me, I shall come looking for you Signor and lock you up!'

'Never saw nothing weird before last night so can't help you inspector,' the elderly plumber sullenly retorted shuffling on his chair, expecting to be let go.

Bruno sighed loudly before finally motioning to the plumber's lawyer that they could both go.

The shuffling exit with extended grumblings on the part of the plumber done, the inspector sat down in the empty opposite chair and pondered his next move in the uncomfortable realisation that the elderly man recently sat opposite was probably telling the truth.

*

Another individual also previously at the site of the concealed corpse was diligently examining what had been prised out from behind the boiler.

Leaning over the body as it lay on the autopsy table and using a bright spotlight mounted on her head and with two sets of tweezers, Patricia Ener picked and prodded at the bullet hole still visible in the back of the skull amidst wisps of faded black hair.

Inspector Bruno and Detective Sergeant Chilabon then entered the room by appointment and were motioned over by the white suited, pony-tailed pathologist, her face covered by a cloth gauze mask.

Bruno quickly introduced his assistant.

Ener replied 'hello' with her veiled head and continued working. satisfied that the inspector was assisted by a female detective sergeant as equally determined to succeed in a man's world as Ener had been. 'You both arrived at just the right time,' she said, pointing at the corpse with the tweezers in her right gloved hand. 'The bullet entered here just below the base of the skull.' She picked up a magnifying glass for a closer inspection. 'I found the bullet lodged deep inside, burning around the hole indicating that the gun was fired from close range. I'll send it for analysis to determine the calibre.'

'Was the body tied up before or after death?' Bruno asked, peering over Ener's shoulder.

'Hard to say,' she replied. 'Because the body is so old precise details will be hard to ascertain. I would say the victim was probably shot elsewhere as there seemed to be a lack of any evidence of extensive blood on the floor. Also the precise path of the bullet makes it seem more like an execution rather the victim having been moving around in a violent manner like on battlefield.'

'Male?' Chilabon asked.

'Can't say yet, inspector. The hair, what's left of it seems too long for a male soldier but it isn't conclusive. Body is partially skeletal and definitely wearing a military uniform that seemed to have been in a good condition when death occurred,' Ener said turning to face the inspector. 'There is a military insignia on the belt,' she said pointing at a piece of faded leather on the belt on a side table. 'There are what seem to be bullet holes in the shirt that may have been inflicted around the time of death. Look,' Ener said pointing with a small torch, 'there are insignia flashes on the collar. It's not a German uniform that's for sure or an allied uniform as far as I can see so it could be a local militia fighter.'

'I am no military historian,' Bruno responded peering at the denuded uniform collar and shirt cuffs. 'But as there seem to be no fascist type flashes on the shirt collar or cuffs I would conclude it was a post 1943 pro-liberation militia soldier attached to the allies.'

*

'What did you think of our new forensic pathologist Mandy?' Bruno asked as they made their way to the police car after taking their leave.

'Like looking in the mirror sir,' Chilabon responded with a smile.

'Ah,' Bruno smiled. 'Another female go-getter! Better than a lazy male slob? Is that the only competition?'

'Pathologist Ener and myself in a little bit of friendly

competition inspector? Why not? We've just started our careers near-as-damit,' Chilabon continued. 'Who will shine? Who will crash and burn?'

'I hope neither of you crashes and burns Amanda!' Bruno said reassuringly as he started the engine. 'Seems like she's doing fine anyway,' he added breezily as they set off back to the station.

'Still she can't say for sure who our man is sadly,' DS Chilabon added.

'That's our job Mandy! She's the pathologist, not a magician.'

Saturday 28 January – 9.25 a.m.

Coming out of *UPIM,* the only high street department store on the Corso that sold clothes he could afford, Ronnie stopped at the newspaper stand outside. The local paper, *Il Centro* was on sale that morning with the grisly *Palazzo Gran Sasso* find as the lead story. Trying to read and understand the story in the bitter cold, he realised help was needed from someone who spoke better Italian than him. His fellow English teacher Bernadette Kenny lived nearby so messaging her, he asked if they could meet in the nearby Caffe Vittorio on the Corso Marrucino?

Bernie worked in Darius' main language school operation further down the Corso and spoke fluent Italian from her Modern Languages degree. As it was the weekend, she duly obliged and in a short while, breezed into the cafe with a smile that forced Tom to smile back.

Petite and always well-dressed, she didn't let her slight frame stop her giving as good as she got from over attentive Italian males that invariably stopped to comment on her; that she could respond in fluent Italian and in local dialect usually shocked them into silence. She put on her rimless glasses as she scrutinised the newspaper report as Ronnie, standing next to her in the queue, ordered two regular cappuccinos with Italian style croissants. They then ambled over to a comfortable leather sofa in the warm interior as winter gusts blew up and down the Corso, giving the cold spot on the stairs to his apartment a run for its money. Which was the coldest, Ronnie mused to himself?

He settled down to listen as Bernie continued.

'It says here in the report the boiler pipes supplied a large apartment used during the war as an informal base in monitoring anti-fascist activities in Chieti. The chief German collaborator, unnamed, would on occasion shoot innocent bystanders on the Corso from the apartment balcony, just to keep up an element of fear among the locals. He was supposed to have disappeared in 1944, so the speculation was that the corpse found behind the boiler was his. The police, the report said, were keeping an open mind while pursuing lines of enquiry.'

'Man alive,' Ronnie shrugged as only an Englishman could, as he stirred his generous cappuccino.

Then putting the white ceramic cup down for a moment on the wrought iron and glass table he wondered if that was indeed the collaborator at the mortuary? 'Wouldn't they have strung him up like Mussolini?' Ronnie wondered, had seen pictures of Il Duce and several others hanging upside down in a Milan square in April 1945. It had to be doubtful that the assistant collaborator would have escaped if his leader hadn't?

'No idea,' Bernie responded. 'There might have been a post-war settling of scores before the allies took over, but no one seems to know,' she finished.

Cabot told her about the cold spot obstructing his path on the stairs, not knowing if she would laugh or commiserate.

Bernie didn't laugh however, but furrowed her brows somewhat and listened seriously.

'There's this batty old cleaner also and she said the corpse they dug up behind my boiler in the basement 'wants justice'.

'Blimey!' it was Bernie's turn to express surprise. 'She reckons it's a *she?*'

'Apparently,' Ronnie replied. 'The old bat already knows something the cops don't then or if they do, aren't saying,'

'Show me this cold spot then please?' Bernie asked, intrigued.

After their drinks in the warm cafe, they donned their scarves and gloves and went over to seek out the offending stair case obstacle. The caretaker was off at weekends so the car park booth was closed.

'Oh my God,' Bernie let out after walking through the icy patch. 'You can really feel it,' she shuddered, looking around for any more evidence of the frosty sentinel.

Ronnie stood watching her as she hopped around the spot in the cold. He quite liked her in her dark stockings but had never asked her what she thought of him. Should he? Would he…?

'You should tell the cops,' she said interrupting his train of thought. 'That Inspector Bruno, why not?'

'Maybe,' was all Ronnie could reply. 'He would never believe me I reckon if I said he should investigate cold spots,' he snorted as they took their noisy leave of the draughty corridor.

The wind continued to swirl around the stone columns that faced the exposed middle part of the palazzo.

Wasn't there just the faintest sound of a cry?

Way up in the air?

*

10.10 p.m.

Later that evening after a few beers in a local bar with a couple of fellow English teachers including Bernie, Ronnie made his way back home.

Strolling into the palazzo, it was only when he had walked up a couple of flights of draughty stairs he realised that the cold spot he had earlier shown Bernie *had disappeared.*

He was so taken aback with this realisation that despite his semi-intoxication, he carefully retraced his steps back to where the cold spot had been, performing then an impromptu jig and subsequently savouring the feeling that it was no more and the aged cleaner could no longer hassle him either.

After lingering at the step in question for a while, Cabot strolled up the flights of stairs in a lighter mood to his apartment.

The apartment keys left *on* the mat signalled that Paolo the plumber had probably been but not put the keys back *under* the mat where Cabot had put them. Ah well, thought Ronnie. The Palazzo Gran Sasso was hardly a crime hotspot, so picking them up he went inside his apartment and closed the door. The radiators were on so after removing his coat, jeans and jumper and plonking them all on his bedroom armchair, he climbed into bed and was soon asleep.

*

A violent knocking at his front door awoke him. He opened the door languidly and there was a young woman with black hair and soft features now standing away from the thresh hold next to the balustrade. She wore a sad expression.

'Who are you? What do you want?'

'I am waiting now,' she calmly responded.

'Waiting for what?' Tom tried to walk towards her but she seemed to move far off.

Then he woke with a start in the darkened room.

Monday 30 January – 8.25 a.m.

After a fitful sleep, Ronnie sat in his kitchen, his feet warmed by the fan heater and pondered his vivid dream.

Who was that woman?

He couldn't get her face out of his mind.

A weary, sad face he considered, but alive enough in those few seconds she had tried to communicate to him.

Then he thought about what the aged cleaner had told him.

'She is waiting.'

'Am I seeing the same person?' he wondered.

On impulse and sober now, he put his coat on and headed off outside down the stairs to where the cold spot had been.

It had really gone, replaced by the ubiquitous smell of a century old palazzo, of stonework, miles of carpeting and a layers of grime in places that had easily defeated an old soldier of clean.

Concluding there was nothing else to see, he walked back to his flat.

At his front door, as he was getting his house key out of his pocket, his attention was suddenly distracted by the faintest of cool breezes, causing him to look to his right towards the corridor balustrade and a frosty palazzo interior in the early morning.

One pace took him in that direction before he suddenly stood still.

Now he was again encased in a freezing pillar of air.

He jumped back with a start, dropping his keys.

The cold spot hadn't disappeared.

It had merely moved to outside his apartment.

*

Inspector Bruno and DS Chilabon were going to the pictures but not to see anything from Rome's premier film studios.

They were at the local library just off the Corso in Chieiti town centre to examine the archives – in particular film taken during the latter stages of the local region and in particular, Chieti's liberation in World War Two.

Bruno had called ahead to ask the library to make available any film taken during the battles to liberate Abruzzo in 1944 – 45, especially the Chieti area.

'We've got some film shot with a cine camera, some copied to video and some photos on microfiche,' librarian Eugenia Spalotti, a woman almost as tall as the inspector with an official air as well as the almost cliché round glasses on a chain around her neck.

'We want to look at any close-up frames of local militia fighters who had assisted the allies and any film of captured German prisoners,' Chilabon explained as Spalotti led them through the central reading area housed in a building not dissimilar to Ronnie Cabot's palazzo building.

In a smaller room off the reading area, a technician had loaded up some newsreel film of the liberation pointed at a small screen in one corner of the room.

Next to the screen was a video player with several videos piled up with film chaotically inscribed with local place-names along with phrases such as "surrender, Lanciano," and "shellfire, Vasto?"

'Wonder, if I'll see my old grandad in one of these shots?' Amanda Chilabon asked.

'Was he involved then?' Bruno enquired as they sat down.

'In part of the fighting in this area but he never said much about it. He was very young then,' she added. 'Your family, sir?'

'No, DS Chilabon,' Bruno replied. 'I only had a grandmother during that time as my grandfather had died of TB. No wonder drugs like penicillin to help them then.'

Bruno and Chilabon then sat waiting as the young male technician dressed in jeans and T-shirt switched the cine film on.

All three then sat and watched for a while as scenes of combatants from both sides were filmed in various stages of battle as well as dead bodies, wrecked military equipment and panning shots of the debris of battle.

'Stop, Paolo stop!' Jordi Bruno jumped up waving his hand in front of the projector.

Paolo the projectionist froze the film as a militia man stood mid shout with his arm pointing at someone off camera. 'Look at his uniform, Amanda!'

Chilabon got out her digital camera and recorded the shoulder flashes on the soldier as well as the distinctive army shirt buttons.

'What uniform's that Paolo do you know?' Bruno asked the young man as he turned the light on and stood waiting by the projector.

'That's an anti-fascist militia uniform inspector,' Bruno replied after surveying the screen with a magnifying glass helpfully supplied by Paolo.

'Pity our film is black and white,' Bruno said, 'but now we have evidence to describe the uniform our body was dressed in DS Chilabon. Can you print me a copy of that shot Paolo please?'

*

Still anxious about the icy presence outside his front door, Ronnie Cabot resumed teaching one of his weekly evening English courses at the enormous Comune or local municipal government building just off the main Corso Marrucino. This imposing baroque building housed the local government offices including the Mayor's office as well as local and national political party branches. Ronnie had been engaged by Darius to teach English to a collection of vaguely interested Christian Liberal Party members on their respective floor of the building.

An 'English lesson' usually meant about an hour of teaching with supplied textbooks before Ronnie and a few of the students retired to the extensive bar and social area next door to the classroom. This was a good opportunity for him to practise his Italian, play backgammon and hear the gossip about Chieti or Italy in general that never appeared in any of the English newspapers.

'We are *called* Christian Liberals,' a grinning Signor Orazio Mancetti told Ronnie as they sat down with local lagers at a green baize table near the bar. A thickset man with masses of black hair and a black beard, Signor Mancetti was the local party secretary with a ready jovial air who always got his round in – something Ronnie admired as a pub *afficionado*. 'But I can tell you this as you are a foreigner, really we are fascists,' he said knotting his eyebrows together and dropping his voice to a whisper.

'What?' Ronnie put his beer down, grimacing in genuine surprise at the dramatic *sotto voce*. 'I don't understand Orazio.'

'It's easy,' Signor Mancetti said draining half of his lager with one gulp – (that would be Ronnie's cue to return to the bar in a few minutes, not that he ever had to *buy* any alcohol at this bar). 'If we told the government we were really an extreme right wing we wouldn't have any of *this*,' he said indicating with his outstretched arm around the tastefully furnished bar room with a suite of attached rooms as evidence.

'True,' murmured a couple more of Cabot's students as they sat down at the table, clutching tall beer glasses with their own lagers.

'We pretend to be liberals,' Mauro Andretti, a middle-aged social worker with greying hair indicated, 'but we still remember *Il Duce*.'

'Doesn't the government know?' Ronnie asked a bit incredulously.

'Sure,' Danielle Entrada, a young female doctor sitting next to him responded. 'No-one cares because the EU sends *all* Italians, what you say, *national and regional subsidies.*'

'Does Darius know?' Cabot asked, his clumsily hidden indignation rising.

'Know? He's a party member!' Orazio said laughing, finishing his lager. 'Another one?' He said, getting up and pointing at Ronnie's empty beer glass.

'Yes, please,' Cabot responded automatically while his brain tried to make sense of what he had just heard. His boss, an unreconstructed fascist?

Cabot liked a man who got his round in though he hadn't previously considered that person's politics a factor in whether he accepted a drink or not?

As the clock crept towards midnight and the bar slowly emptied, Ronnie was having one for the road at the bar as he didn't have to get up early tomorrow morning. Chatting with Mauro, unhappily unmarried it seemed to Ronnie, the English student outlined his new scheme for independent living that may in due course acquire a suitable mate.

Mauro's parents had just bought their son a new apartment

in Citta Sant' Angelo, a nearby hill town not unlike Chieti although on a smaller scale. In fact, Ronnie was going to visit Mauro at his house warming party in a few weeks. Mauro wanted a wife and family though neither he nor his foreign friend had any idea if it would happen. Didn't Catholic Italy still have arranged marriages, Ronnie wondered?

'Left and right politics still exist here,' Mauro was saying earnestly, changing the subject from unrequited love. 'Everyone knows whose side their family was on in the war. When the allies came here in 1945 there was revenge by some people against German collaborators but with you British in control, life went quickly back to normal.'

'Normal?' Ronnie asked, wondering what that looked like in a bankrupt war-ravaged country? Perhaps just no more killing, which would have been a start.

'Next time, you are on the Corso,' Mauro continued, 'look around more carefully.'

'Why?' the Englishman asked finishing his beer and putting an empty glass on the bar. A smaller half pint soon appeared delivered by Simone Ribetti, the agreeable jolly barman. He wasn't studying English but happy enough to keep fellow party members in lager. Ronnie liked it when Simone remembered NOT to speak dialect at him to give him an even chance of understanding what he was saying.

'Because,' Mauro said, putting out his cigarette but careful not to send clouds of smoke in Ronnie's direction as Ronnie had told his students he was asthmatic. 'The, how you say, *emblems*? All from Il Duce's time. Look for the bundle of sticks emblem with an axe. These are fascist symbols.'

'Where?'

Mauro looked at his online dictionary. 'Man-hole covers,

drain covers, commemoration plaques over the theatre, over the cinema on the Corso. Street lights even. The emblem is everywhere.'

'Why didn't anyone change them after the war?

'Imagine the cost?' Mauro replied shrugging his shoulders. 'Italy had no money so getting enough food and repairing ruined buildings in the town was more important for people like my parents than fascist decorations on the buildings.'

Thursday 2 February – Lunchtime

Ronnie Cabot was sitting alone in the Caffe Vittorio on the Corso watching TV at the bar while having a bar baguette.

As it was bitterly cold outside, the large windows fronting the street were all closed and a couple of large fan heaters whirred away from opposite corners of the room. As an ex-public-school boy he had studied Latin which enabled him to recognise many modern-day Italian words though he couldn't follow extended TV dialogues or chat. Instead he followed the live subtitles at the bottom of the screen.

Darius had previously told him that Mussolini had regularised Italian grammar.

Orazio had also told him that fascist Italy had introduced the *Voi* pronoun for *You* plural so people could feel equal and modern. As English used *you* for singular and plural that step hadn't seemed such a big step to an English speaker.

Much of the local Abruzzese dialect however, endured, resonating back to a more old-fashioned Italian, which was why Ronnie had problems following it.

He was reading an English newspaper a friend had brought from Pescara where they were sold at the main railway station. There was a story from Yorkshire, where Ronnie had been born, about flooding which was a big problem in the hilly areas there. A TV reporter had asked a resident how they felt after building flood defences all night? 'Drained,' came the reply, which caused Ronnie to let out a laugh. Other lunchtime punters turned to wonder what the foreigner was doing laughing in their bar.

Ronnie, smirking, looked down in embarrassment.

Just then the local news for Chieti came on the TV and the patrons shifted their gaze from him to it.

Looking up, Ronnie recognised a few of the local report venues while the reporter commented in semi-dialect which made following the story more difficult for him. Palazzo Gran Sasso appeared on the screen with film of the police investigation of the body behind the boiler.

Ronnie sat up and concentrated on the screen. He didn't need Bernie to understand to understand most of the report. Then it was back to the studio with the newsreader introducing a doctor giving a short interview to the press with the Italian subtitles at the bottom of the screen – *'Body discovered in Palazzo Gran Sasso identified as female.'*

Friday 3 February – am

The palazzo maintenance man had an unexpected visitor the next morning as he guided cars in and out of the Palazzo Gran Sasso car park.

A man in a suit came up to him, showed him a newspaper report, then left. This news had the effect of the maintenance man immediately calling someone on his mobile phone and then waiting in his booth for them to show up, regardless apparently of what they were doing. Soon enough, Ronnie was surprised by a knocking at the door of his apartment. Not especially by the knocking but by muffled conversation he could hear from his kitchen table, going on, on the other side of the front door. Putting down his paper and mug of tea and turning down LBC he'd been listening to on the internet, he got up to see what was going on.

He opened the door.

The maintenance man stood there nervously with his flat cap off looking about.

Beside him, a woman in her twenties he surmised, Ronnie's height with short black hair and decked out seemingly with most of the contents of the *Accessorize* shop he had walked past on the Corso on many occasions.

'Hello,' she said with a wide smile, offering a small bony hand to shake. 'My uncle doesn't speak English but wants to come in and look around your apartment, if you don't mind?' Her eyebrows raised, as if they were enough to brush him aside.

'Why?' Ronnie asked, not unreasonably.

Although, her uncle was supposed to be the palazzo maintenance man and caretaker, he wasn't a policeman and in the six months Ronnie had lived in his apartment, he had never taken care of anything apart from the car-park.

Some hurried conversation in local dialect followed, of which Ronnie made out at frequent intervals *'say that...'*

'My uncle, Signor Tomaso Scilaci, wants to look at the pipes and radiator to see if your apartment is properly warm he says. By the way I am Anna Bianca,' she said brightening somewhat and looking straight at Tom. 'You're an English teacher right?'

He said he was, increasingly liking her cheerful demeanour but groaning inwardly towards her uncle. Evidently Anna seemed like another Italian he had met in the space of a few days who had learnt their well nuanced English from elsewhere than suburban Chieti he thought.

There was more to this visit Ronnie suspected than water pipes but agreed to let them both cross the threshold, as much to talk to Anna as anything else.

As soon as Signor Tomaso was in the apartment he moved around like the Duracell bunny while Anna hovered awkwardly in the hall next to the row of coat hooks nailed to the wall and the small half-moon table where Ronnie put the house keys and wallet when he came home. Confirming Ronnie's suspicions, Tomaso had strode straight through the flat, ignoring the antique metal pipes in front of him along the bottom of the apartment walls, and made for the balcony after opening the heavy glass-panelled doors.

Ronnie looked at Anna with furrowed brows and question marks popping out of his head.

She looked back blankly, arms folded, after craning her neck to see what uncle was doing.

Walking through to the living room, they then found Tomaso standing on the balcony but not looking towards the street or across to the other buildings.

Instead, he was looking back *into* the apartment and at the ceiling. He pondered a while, muttering away to himself.

'What's he doing?' Cabot asked Anna. Then before she had a chance to answer, 'Is he going to close the balcony doors? He's making the whole flat cold.'

Ignoring Ronnie, she strode onto the balcony and ordered Tomaso to come back in, and after a hurried apology to Cabot for bothering him, escorted her uncle out of the apartment. As she was about to close the door, she stopped and apologised.

'I am sorry,' she said, 'but this morning a man from the police department told the TV news the female body found downstairs was killed by a 6 mm bullet. This shocked him. You know why?'

'No,' Ronnie confessed, increasingly bewildered by events around him.

'This type of bullet came from Luger pistols,' Anna continued. 'Only German officers or local fascist militia officers carried these during the war. My uncle's aunt was guarding a fascist officer in 1944 when she disappeared.'

'I'll tell you one thing,' Ronnie said not particularly concerned at its implications, 'the old cleaner biddy who supposedly cleans this palazzo told me I had released *her,* she said. It was my fault she said! *She* was released from her torment and now wants revenge!'

Anna stood by the front door, leaning on the handle, temporarily halted in her tracks by Ronnie's revelation. *'Biddy?'* she asked smiling.

Ronnie, his irritation disarmed by her smile, explained.

Hurried conversation with her uncle followed before Ronnie interrupted, 'Perhaps your uncle had better ask the old bat, sorry, cleaning lady, what's going on instead of the police?'

'You'll see,' Anna sighed, smiling lamely and closing the door, though not before leaving her business card which mentioned *English translator* on the hall table.

'Thanks,' he said, not sure if he had really meant it.

*

Lunchtime
'Oh my God, the girl I saw in my dream!'
Ronnie Cabot's mouth opened in shock as he forced himself to put his sandwich down before he dropped it on the cafe floor.

Around him though, no-one else registered any similar reaction while the lunchtime news played on in the background behind the bar.

He had been enjoying a quick ham sandwich, before going to his afternoon classes when his attention was drawn to the enormous TV screen. His palazzo was shown again with a summary he supposed, of the case of the mummified body. The live feed underneath was too quick to follow but the report was accompanied by the head and shoulders portrait of a woman with dark hair dressed in what seemed like a military uniform. 'Disappeared 1944 Francavilla area,' the accompanied subtitle explained.

'Wonder, where the cops got the photo from?' he asked the spirit bottles behind the bar. The ongoing investigation meant that Tomaso, instead of previously ignoring Ronnie because he didn't have a car, now waved at him as if he now were family.

'Caio,' Cabot waved back awkwardly though unable to stop himself smiling.

*

<u>2.55 p.m.</u>

Strangely satisfied as well as intrigued at this outbreak of chumminess at the palazzo, Ronnie arrived to teach his afternoon classes in Chieti Scalo, the industrial and commercial part of Chieti at the bottom of the hill from the historic old town. The Chieti Scalo branch of Darius' little empire was situated in an anonymous two storey office block on the main high street. It gave no hint from the outside as being a hotbed of English language acquisition given the hubbub that occasionally percolated from the open windows upstairs was always Italian.

Ronnie went upstairs and opened the office door.

He was surprised to find Signor Darius Celestini, his employer, in conversation with Tiziana Sangregorio, the school's local secretary.

An affable well-dressed woman in her mid-twenties who manned the office phone and dealt mostly with lesson payments from adult and child English learners as well as engaging with waif and strays who were lured through the doors after seeing posters of Big Ben and Buckingham Palace on the outside windows. As Darius paid Tiziana a signing up fee she was always looking to sign up new English learners of all ages, having convinced them or their parents, that English was the key to their future happiness and fulfilment.

'What was Signor Scilaci doing in your apartment?' Darius asked Ronnie, looking up with his arms folded quizzically.

'How do you know he was in my apartment?' Ronnie asked, taken off-guard.

'I heard,' Celestini replied mysteriously. 'Anyway Ronnie, my question stands.'

54

'Well, he said he wanted to check the pipes and he *is* the caretaker so I thought there was no harm in it,' Ronnie replied not unreasonably.

'There's nothing there for him to check so don't let him in again, okay?' Darius said pointing his finger accusingly at Ronnie. He let this somewhat over the top response from Darius pass on this occasion but was mystified as to why Darius was so worked up about it.

'What shall I say to him then if he asks to come in again?' Ronnie asked looking over Darius' shoulder at his waiting students, all accountants from the state petroleum company '*AGIP*' chatting away in the classroom and oblivious of his presence.

English lessons were for adults like these well turned-out middle-class types, a social occasion as much as a learning one as they were here on company time. Even though practising English wasn't top of the list for them, they were always very polite to Ronnie about it!

'Tell him to go away Signor Cabot!' Darius replied over his shoulder as he was leaving the building.

Tiziana and Ronnie sighed with relief. Darius' twitchy behaviour was out of character and something his employees could do without, they concluded.

'The body seems to be of a woman soldier who disappeared in 1944 according to the TV news and people around me like the palazzo caretaker Scilaci and our great leader have become very *flustered* about it,' he corrected his English to something less slangy so Tiziana could follow him.

A pause while both considered the origins as well as the possible implications of Darius' anxiety.

Tiziana was balanced on the edge of the desk showing a lot

of dark stocking leg Ronnie reflected. Before he had time to reflect further on this pleasing subject, the image of her large, bearded boyfriend Emilio forced its way into Cabot's mind along with Emilio's large fist pounding Cabot's head if he thought Cabot was getting too close.

Ronnie brought his daydream to an end.

'I've had more people *traipsing* – sorry, walking around I mean, in my flat in the past week than in all the months since I moved in,' he confessed, deciding however, not to share with her the ghostly dream he had had.

It wasn't for public consumption.

Neither was the revelation from Orazio Mancetti that Signor Celestini was a fascist sympathiser.

Perhaps Tiziana was one too?

He looked at his watch.

The bell went for the start of the lesson, so after mock-grimacing at Tiziana, Ronnie went and greeted his well-dressed students relaxing and chatting in the airy classroom overlooking the main road.

An hour and a half later, when class was over and having said goodbye to his students, Ronnie went back into the office area and found Tiziana getting ready to lock up and go home.

She pointed at a piece of paper on her desk next to her copy of the local paper. There was Ronnie's palazzo on the front page.

'She called you here on the landline. Can you call her?'

Cabot looked at the message. It was from Anna.

'How did she get this number?' he asked – the second time in one evening he wondered how what he had done or said had become public knowledge? Ronnie continued, 'We can say also in English *"get in touch with,"* – your phrasal verb for the week Tiziana!'

They were both laughing as Ronnie went downstairs and onto the pavement, right, along the street to the tram stop to catch the electric tram which zig-zagged its way up the winding hill road to old Chieti and the Cabot residence. Tiziana however, waited on the pavement for Emilio, who in spite of his bear like stature, occasionally took Ronnie out for a few beers. Tiziana and Emilio both lived in the suburbs of Pescara, a few miles away on the coast.

Monday 6 February – Lunchtime

'*I* sent the black and white photo of the woman to the police who then showed it to the TV company,' Anna confessed as they sat down on Caffe Vittorio's comfortable sofa with double espressos as the lunchtime crowd started to grow. 'Because... my uncle Tomaso,' she continued in a quiet tone as if she were dispensing the secret of some magic trick, 'told me because the body had to be his aunt Margaretta. She disappeared in 1944 in this area but we didn't know about the Francavilla connection. Our family have always wanted to know what happened to her.'

'What did the police say about it being Margaretta?' Ronnie asked turning to face her, spotting an Accessorize necklace in front of her black tea shirt.

Daydreaming again, he wondered if she had a loyalty card for all the trinkets and clothes she'd bought from the store but diplomatically didn't pursue it.

'They then called me and my uncle to the police station,' Anna continued, 'for an interview after they received the photo,' she replied. 'I think they will probably do a DNA test on him and look for a match between them. I am sure though uncle was looking for something obviously in your apartment but I don't know what,' she said crossing her arms and looking to Ronnie for some kind of reassurance that Tomaso was on the right lines.

He smiled back, though rather at a loss how he could reassure her about anything concerning his flat apart from the fact it was warm again with a newly functioning boiler.

He wanted to tell her about his paranormal experience and his dream about Margaretta – he knew her name now – but again was reluctant to share it with anyone. Was it a misplaced sense of loyalty to Margaretta if it were indeed her, trying to communicate with him? Had Tomaso also indeed seen her?

'How did you get the Chieti Scalo number by the way Anna?' Ronnie asked.

'I called Signor Celestini's school on the Corso and asked them where you worked in the evenings – simple!' she said with a shrug.

Ronnie was impressed.

They parted around an hour later as she had a lecture to go to and he had to go back to Chieti Scalo. They had decided however, to meet up again next weekend somewhere down town by the coast. This was Ronnie's initiative and she hadn't demurred. He hardly knew her so he had nothing to lose being in her agreeable company.

Perhaps, he should try and buy something from *Accessorize* too to wear?

Ronnie smiled, thinking the store would probably think he was a weirdo and refuse to serve him.

He checked his mobile phone after she had left.

There was a message from Darius repeating his order not to let Tomaso back in his apartment.

He sent an "okay" reply.

*

10.20 p.m.
Arriving home from work quite late that evening, Ronnie Cabot saw that the door to the apartment opposite his was ajar. He had

heard that a slightly dotty old woman who spoke excellent English lived there. Having never met her or ever seen any activity near her apartment, he drew near his door and while fiddling with a set of house keys that clinked sharply in the cold night air, heard a shrill, 'Come in,' in an elderly female voice emanating from beyond the front door.

Gingerly, he walked over the thickly carpeted hallway cluttered, he thought, with too many pictures on the corridor wall and decorative tatty furniture.

'In here!' the voice shouted.

He entered a bright living room area, smaller than the dimensions of his own one the other side of the dividing wall. Sitting in a red leather armchair watching TV was a sprightly elderly woman; well dressed and holding a large sherry glass in one hand with a cigarette holder in the other.

'Will you have one?' she enquired.

'Thanks,' he replied not sure if she was offering a cigarette or a drink.

She pointed to the drinks table in the corner.

It was up to Cabot to sort himself out.

'I am Contessa di Lanciano,' she replied, smoking and leaning back in her armchair. 'I heard on TV about the poor girl they found downstairs.'

'I'm Ronnie Cabot,' he said, then adding rather limply, 'Yes, it's terrible,' before sitting down on an opposite armchair in response to a beckoning of the Contessa's hand. She must have followed the events closely, he thought. He needed more data on the Contessa though before he could decide whether she was friend or foe.

Small talk followed as the Contessa questioned Ronnie about his background, listening attentively as he told her about public school and working in a West African high school before she brought the subject back to what *she* evidently wanted to discuss.

'A terrible business,' she said continuing with Ronnie now listening politely. 'But, you see, the war brought out the worst in a lot of people living here. Some resisted,' she added, 'and some supported the German and Italian pact as the way forward.'

She finished her sherry with one last unladylike gulp and a look of glee on her parched face.

As a foreigner, before he had come to live in Chieti, Cabot knew very little about the second world war as it was fought in Italy beyond having watched Rossellini's *'Rome Open City.'* He knew nothing about the 1944 – 45 German defence of Abruzzo, aided and abetted by a determined local fascist militia. No books in English or TV programmes had ever mentioned it.

'It seems to me that the war hasn't entirely gone away then, for some people,' the Englishman ventured, remembering what Orazio had told him at the Comune about masked political affiliations.

'You work for Signor Darius Celestini, *little star* in your language,' she said filling up her glass from a bottle on a side table previously hidden from her guest and motioning him over to the dummy waiter behind him to do the same. '*He* has prospered, but I won't say more. Walls have ears, you English say,' she said furtively.

Ronnie thought it unlikely anyone was bugging this old soul but she seemed to know more than she was letting on.

'Why are you telling me this? he asked.

'You English, you are so, how you say, accommodating.' the Contessa said with a smile. 'You all try to see the best in everyone but here there are old memories and old people like me to carry them. However, I too am old and no one cares what I think,' she said. 'But I *know* you don't need to go far to solve this mystery,' she finished up, shaking her empty sherry glass at the floor in the general direction of the hidden tomb fifty feet or so below.

Ronnie remained outwardly nonplussed at her statement however, wondering if it just the sherry talking? 'Well Signor Celestini is my boss and pays my wages *and* it's his apartment so I am leaving it to him and the police to find the truth Signora,' Cabot replied finishing his sherry at length and getting to his feet ready to leave.

'Goodbye and take care,' she said with a half a laugh, offering a bony hand by way of gratitude for him spending a few minutes with her, in a probably lonely world, Cabot speculated.

'Close the door please on your way out,' her voice drifted down the draughty corridor to her front door.

Having had two large sherries, perhaps he did take a bit longer getting his front door key out again.

The sherry blanket though couldn't shut out a realisation that took hold of him.

The cold spot had disappeared from outside his door.

Performing another impromptu jig around the threshold, he carefully waving his arms out looking for a cold blast of air apart for the winter draughts that normally swirled about the corridors, open to the elements as they were on one side.

Nothing.

Now then!

He closed his door and went inside and straight to his bedroom overlooking the street.

Attracted by a bright light in his peripheral vision, he turned to look at the doors by the bedroom balcony.

The female figure stood there, not six feet away, wrapped in a shimmering dark uniform. She was staring at him with penetrating eyes and pointing to the ceiling.

Ronnie, momentarily paralysed, stepped back in shock, his mouth falling open.

'Tell me, what you want for Christ's sake!' he blurted out before retreating clumsily to the gloomy living room.

Tuesday 7 February – Seven Thirty a.m.

The next morning, unshaven and irritable, Ronnie got up, still dressed, from the living room sofa where he had spent an uncomfortable night after the eerie encounter in his bedroom a few hours earlier.

The winter sun flooded into the whole apartment, banishing the gloom and temporarily, the unsettling memories the Contessa had warned him about.

He washed his face and had a shave, determined to be brave towards whatever had been released by the discovery in the boiler room.

Putting his head cautiously round his bedroom door for some clean clothes, he saw that the room was now empty and the morning sun flowed in through the balcony doors.

'It' had gone.

'What the hell was she pointing at?'

As intriguing to Ronnie as the spectre's appearance was what a Contessa was doing living in a poky flat?

Weren't they supposed to live in grand mansions?

Cabot walked back into the living room, thoughtful, lips pressed together as he gathered his thoughts.

A few minutes later, with a fresh brewed coffee in hand, he sat down at the small kitchen table and reflected on what had occurred.

The radio was on now bringing news from back home.

Text messages flew back and forth between him and Anna

as he decided to tell her what he had witnessed. Hard to believe that only a few feet away through thick palazzo brickwork the Contessa's *mini-palazzo* was situated, full of clutter from floor to ceiling…

'From floor to ceiling,' he turned over in his mind as he contemplated the comparative emptiness of his apartment…

A pause.

His mouth opened slowly as he leaned back, comprehension of the absurdly simple taking over his brain.

'Can it really be?' he asked out loud, before jumping up with his hands in the air, his fingertips barely touching the whitewashed ceiling.

*

Ronnie tried to call Inspector Bruno with his new idea, but finding he was unavailable and unwilling to leave a message, finished the call.

Deciding next that it was time he went to see Darius Celestini in his office in the town centre, he set off to the Corso Marrucino as soon as he had finished his bacon sandwich, Italian style and second freshly brewed coffee.

Seeing the aged cleaner in the corridor with her metal bucket, he hazarded a greeting to announce his presence as he suspected she was a bit deaf as well as preparing her for some bad Italian.

'The cold spot has disappeared yes?' he asked a slowly turning head and mop. 'First she was *here*,' he said pointing to the stairs he had just descended. '*Then,* she went to my front door. *Now*,' he waited for a dramatic pause as the cleaning lady squinted somewhat incredulously at the mad foreigner's outburst,

'*I saw her in my bedroom doing this,*' he finished up, imitating her pose, which he realised was not that dissimilar to the Statue of Liberty's pose in New York harbour.

Another pause.

'*Madonna,*' old lady replied crossing herself and then a long burst in Italian without any punctuation as far as Ronnie could make out.

He nodded, smiling as he reminded himself of his clever deduction as he made his way to the Corso.

*

'Why is the ceiling in my apartment lower than my neighbour's Signor Celestini?' Ronnie asked in a casual voice once he was directed to settle in a comfy armchair in Darius' somewhat cluttered office.

Darius' private school building, the *Language Institute* was another large Baroque palazzo style building further down the Corso than Ronnie Cabot normally ventured, even on his *passeggiatta*. Considering what had transpired however, Cabot preferred to see his employer face to face rather than trying to relay events over the phone. 'The Contessa's ceiling is about a metre higher I reckon,' he continued filling the space as Darius had said nothing in reply. 'One of them has surely been altered. I'm guessing it's mine,' Ronnie finished up.

Darius had listened quietly but as soon as Cabot mentioned the Contessa, started to shuffle nervously in his seat, his hands resting on his legs.

'She told me she…' Ronnie continued.

'Don't believe anything that old sherry bottle told you,' he said interrupting Ronnie with surprising vitriol that Cabot

66

decided not to finish his sentence. Darius still hadn't answered Cabot's first question about the ceiling so Ronnie decided to tell him about the strange vision; about how the entity had moved location twice through the palazzo from the steps onto the Corso to his bedroom; about how all this had started after the body had been found behind the boiler.

Darius stared hard, his beady eyes focused and arms folded as Ronnie told his story.

What was he thinking? Cabot wondered. What an idiot I am?

'You *saw* her?' he asked finally without any hint of jeering or disbelief. Darius continued to look straight at Ronnie while he outlined his story.

'Yes,' he replied.

'She pointed *upwards*?'

'Yes.'

Darius stood up out of his chair with furrowed brows, hands deep in pockets – unusual behaviour for Ronnie's employer, he considered for a man dressed in an expensive suit.

Darius then turned his back on Cabot and contemplated the view from the window, hands now out of pockets and resting on the dark wood window sill.

The sounds of the Corso drifted over and vied for his attention from the depths of Darius' brain where his cognitive skills seemed to be at work.

He offered no further comment so Ronnie continued talking to his employer's back. 'I tried to phone the police but the inspector was unavailable. 'So, I am leaving it up to you but I want you to put me in another apartment until this has been sorted out.'

'Yes, fine,' Darius said immediately turning round to face him.

Ronnie was a bit surprised by the speed of Darius' response, expecting a bit of a moan about unnecessary costs he was being put to.

'By the way, who did you tell about your ceiling theory?'

'No one so far but Tomaso seemed very interested in it, come to think of it, when he showed up with his niece the other day,' Ronnie replied. He didn't tell Darius about the old cleaner's pronouncements, doubting Darius would take her seriously. 'What will you do now?' Cabot asked.

A pause.

'I will talk to you later,' Darius replied, his mind elsewhere obviously. 'Now, please go back to work and let me deal with this. I will sort out a new apartment very close to the Corso for you.'

Ronnie then got up, expressed thanks and left.

*

Five thirty p.m.

After finishing his afternoon English lessons for somewhat bored local teenagers in Chieti Scalo, Ronnie popped outside to a local take-away which served the best rolled up pizza slices in the area. Anna texted him while he was in the queue to be served, asking if she could meet him at his apartment before his evening classes. He was taking the tram home for a few hours before evening lessons started anyway so he texted back for her to come round.

*

Thinking also he had nothing to lose, Cabot decided to also tell Anna about his spectral visitor once they were sat down in his living room – how it had started as a cold spot which moving progressively towards his apartment culminated in his late-night encounter. A closer understanding between them was evident he concluded, in the fact that she didn't laugh at him initially, but getting up, carefully went over to the balcony doors, looking all around her.

'Yes…' she said slowly to Ronnie's surprise. 'I too can *feel* things,' she confessed, looking up at the low ceiling intently as Ronnie let her into the enigma of the different ceiling levels between his apartment and the Contessa's. 'You see I study philosophy and am a constructionist. I think you are too. If you were a deconstructionist I would have realised the first time we met and we would not be friends.'

Ronnie laughed as he bluffed a deep comprehension of her philosophical bent but inwardly he had no idea what she was talking about. Anna didn't seem too upset when he subsequently confessed this so he went and constructed some real coffee in his little kitchen. Her uncle then called her on her phone and an extended dialogue in dialect followed.

Cabot couldn't follow it all but Anna soon filled him in as she sat in his single worn black armchair in the living room with a careworn expression which made Ronnie immediately feel sorry for her.

'My uncle was talking about Margaretta disappearing at the end of the war…'

'Somebody murdered her and then hid her body,' Ronnie interrupted, 'and that person used a Luger.'

'My uncle never used to think about his aunt very much,' she continued, sipping her coffee in the living room as Ronnie sat down on the single wooden chair with his. He then brought out his shortbread biscuits for their little feast and proffered one to her opposite. 'My uncle never mentioned her to me before the plumber found the body. But now, he wants the police to find out the truth about his poor aunt, even after all these years.'

He posed two questions to himself while she prattled on – was he really a constructionist? More importantly how could it help him get the girl?

Wednesday 8 February – Late Morning

Darius was as good as his word as Ronnie Cabot was now settling into a smaller first floor apartment with a little balcony overlooking the little *Piazza Citalavella,* with the ancient Roman amphitheatre ruins about a hundred yards further down in the historic centre of Chieti.

Darius had sent a van round to the *Palazzo Gran Sasso* first thing in the morning, with a couple of hired helps to move Cabot's possessions and some furniture into his new apartment. Finally thanking Darius' movers and offering a tip, Ronnie closed the front door and sat down in his small living room overlooking the little piazza.

It was somewhat gloomier than his previous apartment due to the fact that the interior walls were painted in a grubby shade of light green.

Sitting in a tatty dark green armchair, he scrutinised his somewhat limited book collection he had carefully brought over from England and afterwards rescued from dust and grime from a partly demolished ceiling.

An eclectic reader of history and mystery amongst other subjects, he read to find out, though generally what he found out satisfied him alone.

No one else he knew cared whether the Germans could have broken through at Prokhorovka in 1943 or not?

No one else he knew cared why King Harold had lost control of his soldiers when William the Conqueror's cavalry pretended to retreat?

71

Indeed, were the Easter Island statues built by a pre-ice age civilisation? No one except him ruminated about them.

Did Richard Quest on CNN ever fly economy in his business show?

Big questions.

No one else he knew or cared but being a deep thinker by nature, especially when sitting by himself in the cafe down the street, passers-by oblivious of the foreigner gazing out of the window.

His ideal spouse was someone who was pretty and even better, had an opinion on the above imponderables?

A cold beer in one hand helped him survey the quiet scene outside though only minutes away from the busy Corso Marrucino. Signor Darius had even bought him a new ironing board and iron still in their wrapping paper. Wonders never ceased!

One thought played on his mind.

Had anyone or *anything* followed him from his old apartment?

Thursday 9 February – 9.25 p.m.

That evening Ronnie was back at the Comune building teaching his regular midweek evening class. Tradition was duly followed by him then retiring to the bar with several of his students including Orazio and Mauro to drink and play cards. Ronnie told them of his recent move following his spooky encounter with the woman in the old photograph whose remains had been lately uncovered.

Maybe because he was their foreign teacher, his little audience listened respectfully and possibly in shock, in contrast to the noise and music from the jukebox and chat around them.

'I know what I saw,' Cabot said finishing up. 'That apartment holds the key to her murder somehow.'

Signor Orazio frowned with his elbows on the table – it satisfied Cabot that they were not laughing at him, whatever their apparent lack of belief in anything they couldn't see. Indeed, he had visited some rural Catholic churches out in remoter parts of Abruzzo and experienced an almost paranormal atmosphere within some, encountering the blood of Christ freshly repainted on large crucifix statues whose eyes really did follow you round the room. Whispered dialect drifted round the table while Ronnie was shot reassuring gestures and fresh lagers appeared indicating he was among friends whatever they were discussing.

'A lot of bad things happened during the war like I told you,' Orazio said sighing. 'Do the police know about the ceiling?'

'I tried to call them but the inspector wasn't there. Darius knows though.'

Friday 10 February – 9.53 p.m.

It was Bernie who burst Ronnie's crowded thought bubble a day or so later when she called him on his phone after evening classes were finished. He was in Chieti Scalo's railway station bar down the street from the language school offices, lager in hand, watching a local football match with one of his students, Bernardo d'Avenzano who was the railway station manager. Putting his beer down, Ronnie went outside to the street where he could hear Bernie better on his phone away from the noise of the football.

'I heard from the school secretary that police went to your old flat after the Contessa had called them. The old caretaker was in there making a hole in your old bedroom ceiling!'

'A hole?' Cabot replied shocked. 'Did they say why?'

'I don't know why but there was a big row between her and Tomaso so when the police arrived, he was arrested for criminal damage,' Bernie said.

*

Ronnie's question to Bernie was answered after barely sitting down at the bar and picking up his lager. Anna was on the line now so once again Cabot apologised to Bernardo and went outside to the pavement.

Bernardo's permanent hang-dog expression resulting from being a harassed single parent with precocious teenage daughters followed him out of the door. He did do Ronnie one favour though, introducing him to "The Alan Parson's Project," whose album *"Eye in the sky,"* was played to death on Bernardo's portable CD player in his station office. Soon the same tunes were drifting out across the Piazza Citalavella.

'When my grandfather got the DNA result from the police telling him it was my great aunt Margaretta they had found behind the boiler, my uncle walked straight out of our apartment and went over to your old apartment, without telling anyone,' Anna sighed down the phone. 'he must have let himself in with a spare key he had kept, gone to your old room where you saw *her* and decided that was where he wanted to look.'

'The ceiling?'

'Yes. Anything he thought may be hidden there that could help him find out what had happened to his aunt?' Anna continued. 'But he made so much noise with this crowbar he had the Contessa heard him and called the police. My uncle is at home now as the police told him not to go back to work.'

'Did he find anything?'

'Well, by the time the police arrived, there was a heap of junk on the floor apart from the wooden ceiling slats, broken plaster and a ton of dust. The policeman told me this as they dropped him off at home. He did however take a couple of things without telling the police…'

Anna's house phone went off interrupting her conversation. Putting down her mobile, a muffled Italian conversation ensued in the near vicinity of Ronnie's ear. Then, 'Inspector Bruno's been trying to contact you,' she replied.

'I tried to call him earlier at the police station,' he told Anna. 'Your uncle should give anything he found to the police and not keep them,' Ronnie advised her. 'It could be very important.'

Anna had no time to respond to Tom's comment as Bruno was then ringing Tom's mobile. Relieved that his English was intelligible over the phone Cabot accepted Bruno's invitation to come down to the police station as soon as possible. He even promised to send a car to Chieti Scalo to collect him.

Ronnie quickly sent a text back to Anna to see if she still wanted to meet up tomorrow.

She agreed and pointed out a cafe in Pescara town centre where they could meet for lunch tomorrow.

Monday 13 February – Ten a.m.

Darius stood in what had been Ronnie's living-room next to a stepladder and torch he had borrowed from the palazzo's maintenance office on the ground floor. Above him, a black hole a couple of feet square where Tomaso had lately been making the ceiling cavity before part of it had fallen on him. He wondered if the Contessa knew he was there. He had tried to be as quiet as the proverbial church mouse. The less he had to deal with her the better.

Gingerly, he climbed up the stepladder and pointed his torch into the darkened spaces shut off from bright winter sunshine outside. Nothing.

The space was empty.

But it hadn't always been apparently.

Darius's torch highlighted drag marks and scuffs in the dusty ceiling interior surface.

What had Tomaso found earlier? he wondered. The Contessa? The police? What about them?

Climbing down the stepladder, he examined a clutter of broken plasterboard fragments and fragments of carpet on the laminated wooden floor left behind by the police. With thumb and forefinger, he picked up dusty carpet pieces and opening the balcony doors, shook them outside, emitting a great cloud of dust and grime.

He started to sneeze as his anger increased. Half of Chieti had traipsed through his bloody apartment in the past four days.

He needed to know what was going on.

Tuesday 14 February – 8.47 a.m.

Inspector Giordano Bruno showed Ronnie into his slightly old-fashioned office in the central police station in the middle of Chieti. Not seeing a computer or laptop on his desk in Ronnie's eyes, a *sine qua non* to successful police work, made him worry if this inspector knew what he was doing? However, Cabot was sensible enough to reserve judgment.

Small-talk was kept to neutral niceties as coffee was ordered from the police station's uniformed dispenser of coffees and snacks and swiftly delivered to the inspector's desk.

'How are you settling into your new apartment?' the policeman politely enquired, dressed in another expensively tailored-suit. His sincere tone certainly impressed his visitor. A copper who cared.

'Fine, thanks,' Cabot replied, happily reporting that there didn't seem to be any mysteries attached to his new residence.

'Well, after the body was identified by DNA as Tomaso's aunt, I was considering how to continue my investigation when two things happened. Signor Tomaso went and dislodged this,' handing Ronnie a dusty faded leather-bound book, 'when he was making a hole in your old apartment ceiling. I also got an interesting letter from your country,' he continued sitting opposite Cabot in a comfortable leather chair in front of a solid dark wood desk strewn with files with a little collection of small photos in silver frames. Opposite Bruno's desk, the far wall was adorned with a photo of the Italian President and the national flag.

Ronnie opened the old book and saw the title in Italian in faded blue ink. He looked up at Bruno.

'*Daily diary actions of the anti-fascist militia in the Chieti area 1944,*' Bruno helpfully translated from the faded Italian script. 'Can you see the entry for 10 August ,' he said.

Cabot scrutinised the entry but the near illegible script defeated him.

Inspector Bruno, standing behind him now, took the book off him, produced a magnifying glass from under a file on the desk and read aloud. 'Major Aldo Molina identified by anti-fascist militia attached to a British and Canadian motorised division as a fascist commander for the Chieti area captured in battle. Ordered by allied command to be separated from main group of prisoners and be driven from Francavilla to Sulmona for interrogation.' Then he read a post-script at the bottom of the page in a different hand, 'Transport disappeared – two anti-fascist militia missing plus prisoner – search underway.'

Well then, why would that be hidden in your ceiling I wonder?' he continued, still standing next to Ronnie, hands folded behind his back. 'Then before long I get this.' He gave Cabot a crisp blue envelope, posted from the UK with a return address in spidery writing on the back.

Inspector Bruno moved to the other side of his desk, hands concealed under paperwork like a poker player protecting his winning hand. 'The discovery of the body next to your boiler got into the English language magazine for foreigners in Pescara and somehow the article got republished in a newspaper in England,' he said then taking two espressos off a tray a junior policeman had brought noiselessly into the room. He indicated to Ronnie to take his. 'This is where it gets more interesting,' the inspector said holding up his right-hand index finger like a priest ready to pronounce the blessing.

Ronnie took the letter from Bruno's left hand and settled

79

back into his chair, putting the coffee on the small table next to him. 'Can I read it?' he asked, focusing on the spidery scrawl on light blue writing paper.

'Please do,' Bruno said, looking over his shoulder through the large bay windows that overlooked the Corso.

'To whom it may concern,' the letter opened.

'I am the regimental archivist for the 8th Berkshire infantry who fought with the allied army liberating Abruzzo in Italy in April 1944. I was contacted by a relative of a veteran who noticed a story in the paper about a body discovered in a building in Chieti that was connected to the battles of 1944. I consulted the regimental diary for those days and it appeared that a Major A.J.P. Edwards sent two anti-fascist fighters on a mission to take a captured fascist commander who called himself Major Molina to headquarters to be interrogated. The jeep never arrived in Sulmona at regimental headquarters and despite a search his men were unable to find the jeep or any trace of the occupants. The war moved to Pescara further north and though the incident was noted in the army record, it seems to have been soon forgotten. I sincerely hope that the regiment... and here Ronnie stopped reading as all heads in the room were turned towards raised voices downstairs.

'Inspector?' Ronnie hesitated with apprehension, 'the Contessa told me that the answer to the mystery wasn't far away.'

'Really,' his eyebrows raised, one ear trying to follow what was going on downstairs. 'How would she know that I wonder? Unless she was connected to it?' he allowed himself a small chuckle at the sheer absurdity of the suggestion.

'I don't know but it seems unlikely she would lie,' Cabot continued, 'but Signor Celestini called her a sherry bottle. Why do they hate each other I wonder?'

'I don't know but I have to ask you officially Signor Cabot

but have you heard your employer's name mentioned in the Comune at any time?'

'Actually I have,' Ronnie replied sighing, not knowing its implications. 'My student, the Christian Liberal Party Secretary told me Signor Darius was a party member.'

'Is he?' Bruno mused slowly, sitting back in his chair. 'Hm.'

Ronnie half smiled in response but before he had time to ruminate further, raised voices and shouting suddenly increased several notches.

Inspector Bruno, his Sergeant, Ronnie and other officers hurriedly made their way to the station's main reception area.

There was Signor Tomaso Scilaci being restrained against the wall by a burly station sergeant who manned the main desk, the first point of call for people walking into the police station off the Corso.

'What's going on Sergeant Degrelli?' Bruno shouted, marching over and grabbing Tomaso's arms and pulling them towards him as another officer handcuffed the agitated, shouting suspect.

'He knows who killed my aunt!' Tomaso hissed.

'Who?'

'That bastard Celestini!' Tomaso shouted, his strength and anger rapidly diminishing as he was forcibly sat on a wooden bench next to the wall.

'He just marched in and demanded to make a complaint,' Degrelli replied breathlessly at length to Bruno's question. 'I asked him what he was talking about but he just started shouting and getting more upset.'

Now Scilaci was sat in handcuffs with Bruno and his officers surrounding him.

Tomaso had become almost childlike now as he wept quietly.

'Don't worry Signor Tomaso,' Bruno said, his anger towards this old man rapidly diminishing. He laid a comforting hand on Tomaso's shoulder, 'I told you before to let me find out the truth behind the body and who is responsible but you can't just walk in here shouting accusations.' He stood up, patted down his dark suit, wondering whether he should press charges against the man who sat subdued in front of him.

It was a short think.

'Up you get signor and off you go. I am not charging you with anything this time okay?' Bruno had deliberately not asked him however if he had handed over everything he had found in the attic space, beyond giving him a reproving look which he hoped had been duly noted.

The main reception area then returned to a more peaceful existence as Station Sergeant Filipo Degrelli took up his place once more behind the desk ready to deal with hopefully more reasonable members of the public needing to talk to him.

Ronnie, still stood by the main desk trying to make sense of the new turn of events.

Whatever Tomaso had found poking around in the ceiling hiding space should be declared, he thought. He said nothing to Bruno about what Anna had said though inwardly though he knew he should have.

'We shall continue our investigations into the Palazzo Gran Sasso so for now you may go,' Bruno told Cabot quietly as Cabot picked up his jacket to go home.

*

3.04 p.m.

'Why would the Palazzo Gran Sasso caretaker think you know who killed his aunt?' Inspector Jordi Bruno asked Darius Celestini in the latter's office later that day. 'Any ideas?'

'No to both!' Darius replied emphatically sitting behind his desk. 'I am a victim here too. One of my apartment ceilings has been damaged by that idiot. Who's going to pay for that?'

'You own the Palazzo Gran Sasso I understand?' Bruno asked sitting in one of the leather chairs in front of Darius' desk and facing him directly, arms folded, looking for evidence of surprise on the man opposite's face.

There was none.

'Yet, written proof is hard to find in the official channels. I had to ask Rome for help in establishing this. Where is the land deed registration? When *did* you come to own the palazzo signor?' Bruno fired the questions like torpedoes hoping for a hit somewhere on the good ship Celestini.

Darius though was still afloat with an inscrutable expression after all he had heard the inspector enquire.

'After the war,' Darius informed the inspector, 'like many people, my late father returned home to Abruzzo and bought the empty palazzo off the allied government I think. He did nothing wrong and no one questioned this at the time.'

'Really?' Bruno replied, leaning forward in his leather chair with one elbow resting on Darius' desk.

The obvious point that Darius had not declared *which* side his father had been fighting on was left hanging. Bruno saved that line of questioning for now as it could cause Celestini to clam up entirely.

Darius, however, was becoming agitated at Inspector Bruno's questioning, but needed to placate this insufferable man. 'I have official deeds somewhere...' he mumbled sullenly. He didn't like being put on the spot by this preening peacock who called himself *Inspector.*

'I'd like to see them,' Inspector Bruno asked with some restraint, his tall frame now leaning over to the opposite sitter, who seemed more like a hobbit than a human. 'I'm not accusing you of anything signor as the events I am asking you about relate more to your father I think. My question is why a nobody like Major Molina, eh… have you heard of him?' Bruno casually enquired.

A blank look met his stare.

'How would a man like this supposedly disarmed Major,' Bruno continued, 'apparently overpower the two escorts and end up maybe burying one of them in the *Palazzo Gran Sasso* when he was supposed to be driven to Sulmona, in the opposite direction?'

'Sulmona?' Darius sat up squarely. 'How do you know he was being taken there?'

*

Signorina Anna Bianca sat down at her desk in her room at Pescara University and got out the grubby little beige cloth bag her uncle had given her and put it on the table.

Opening it, she tipped out a pair of flat little metallic rectangles with small lettering etched into them.

Dog tags with numbers punched into them.

She picked up a small magnifying glass and carefully cleaned the dirty metallic surfaces. In a few seconds the lettering became clearer.

Testaladi Maglio serial number Private
Margaretta Embriaco serial number Private

She stared with a slight awe at the small objects obviously retrieved from bodies and hidden by someone in an anonymous ceiling space. Her uncle had been too afraid to open the bag but she had. He needed to know his aunt's military tags had been found and her fellow soldier's. She picked up her phone and dialled.

*

Inspector Bruno took his leave of Darius Celestini's office without answering Darius' last question concerning Sulmona and walked back to the police station not far down the Corso.

Passing the great medieval Romanesque cathedral of Chieti he reflected on the decision he had taken early on in his life, and to the quiet contentment of his parents.

Namely, that if man was the supreme arbiter of justice in the secular world he had found himself in, then Jordi Bruno would help his fellow man (and woman) dispense that justice.

A higher moral God-given code of living was also available to those who sought it, whatever their walk of life including the police.

Purgatory for sinners in the next world was a concept a man like Jordi Bruno would dismiss as delusional.

However Bruno also needed to threaten criminals with purgatory in this world – at Pescara prison in particular.

He spied the sculptured saints standing sentinel at the tops of the flying buttresses.

Was it his imagination or were they smiling at him directly? If Chieti's top cop had everyone's back fighting crime then maybe these saints and apostles would have *his?*

Bruno checked his watch.

He had time enough to pop into the cathedral, cross himself and light a candle for the eternal repose of the lost soul lately unearthed, by a local plumber. Though he couldn't really explain why, lighting a candle felt an appropriate expression of memory and prayer for a soul lately gathered unto God's keeping.

It would greatly please his parents too.

*

85

Leaving the cathedral after a few minutes, he picked up his pace once again on the Corso and arriving back at his office, picked up his phone and asked the police switchboard to put him through to the Pescara local governmental authority at the Comune. He needed someone to find proof of his suspicion that Darius was lying about his father not having any connection to the palazzo until after the war. Their office may be able to help him search the municipal archives.

*

Darius Celestini also stepped onto the Corso Marrucino.

Nothing of note in that particularly but his itinerary didn't include visiting the cathedral.

Going over to the Chieti Comune during working hours with an agitated air, definitely was, though.

In a quiet albeit restrained voice upon arrival at the general reception area on the ground floor, he demanded to speak immediately with the Christian Liberal Party Secretary, Ronnie's student Signor Orazio Mancetti.

A few eyebrows were raised however, by this fraught behaviour.

Darius was well-known of course. A successful local businessman with business and property interests throughout the Chieti area. He was, however, something of an enigma too with no immediate family apparently and considering how rich he was, lived modestly in an apartment overlooking the sea in the small coastal resort of Termoli, down the coast.

One of the party's secretarial clerks Darius encountered, was Inspector Bruno's girlfriend.

Ella Frantoni, an elfin looking woman with fair hair and freckles.

Ella and Jordi had met at a Catholic singles weekend retreat in the Apennine mountains a few years ago but their relationship was kept discreet for the professional and personal safety of both parties as both of their employers would take a dim view of someone working within their midst with possibly divided loyalties. Ella decided on this occasion however, that her boyfriend should be made of aware of Darius' unannounced, agitated visit.

However in her haste to call him, she forgot, or more probably, wasn't aware, that in calling an external number, her call was flagged up to her supervisor, Signora Michele Ceresa who made a note of the number Ella had dialled and informed the party secretary.

*

Anna heard the bad news from her uncle as she came out of a lecture and immediately called Ronnie. She felt confident confiding in him, further considering inviting him over to her room in the student halls of residence.

'Sorry, he lost his job,' Ronnie said genuinely sad on the phone later with her as he sat in Caffe Vittorio with a lager after work.

'He is very upset and says it's *her* fault,' Anna said sadly. Any future employment in what was a small town where everyone knew everyone was going to be hard if Darius put the word out.

'Whose fault?' Cabot asked.

'That Contessa di wherever,' Anna angrily replied. 'Why couldn't she leave him alone?'

'Come on Anna, he was making loud noises knocking a hole

in the ceiling next door to where she was, and she never goes out,' he responded. He didn't owe Anna anything but tried to get her to see what had happened from his ex-neighbour's viewpoint.

He wasn't succeeding, however. 'Inspector Bruno's got a military diary in Italian which documents your great aunt's war mission and a letter from England,' he continued, 'with an English soldier's account of your great aunt's orders to escort a fascist officer to Sulmona and her disappearance afterwards along with her fellow soldier and the prisoner. Inspector Bruno says he is investigating further,' Ronnie informed her to trying to demonstrate that the police were still interested in solving the mystery.

'I got a chance to have a look at what uncle found,' Anna said quietly. 'You know what was there? Military dog tags.'

'What?' Cabot's eyebrows shot up. 'You have to tell the police Anna,' he said. 'This is serious.'

'No, we're not going to because we don't trust them. Too many people sympathise with the old ideas even today. They don't care about his aunt. You won't tell anyone will you?' she asked hopefully.

'Inspector Bruno isn't like that but you must be honest with him,' Ronnie pleaded with a sigh.

*

Late that night, the aged cleaner looked out of her tiny garret room in the palazzo attic just as a figure with long black hair and long brown coat was standing outside in the corridor next to Ronnie's old apartment.

Who was visiting at that time of night she wondered? Her old eyes watered up in the cold so she could not make out what

88

the figure was carrying but could see enough to realise that it wasn't Ronnie Cabot's empty flat the figure was entering.

A muffled scream resonated throughout the Palazzo Gran Sasso.

Wednesday 15 February – Nine a.m.

'Inspector, please remember you are a public servant. My party members also pay your salary,' Christian Liberal Party Secretary Mancetti reminded Jordi Bruno over the phone the following day.

'Yes and my taxes pay your salary so we are equal so don't threaten me,' Bruno replied in irritated tone, sitting in his office chair.

'Just remember Inspector, Signor Darius Celestini is a respected local businessman. You are harassing him without any evidence!'

'My case is proceeding,' Bruno persisted, 'but unless you get off the phone and let me do my job, I shall issue an official regional order with a copy sent to Pescara to open your party accounts to my office's scrutiny. I will inspect your tax returns personally with the aid of state experts. Do I make myself clear?'

'Leave Signor Celestini alone!'

The phone went dead.

Ella Frantoni warning her boyfriend that Darius and Orazio had had a hurried meeting subsequent to Bruno's questioning of Darius meant Inspector Bruno was then ready to fend off any attempt to scupper his investigation of an old murder on the property of a local businessman with ties to the ruling party. Still, the inspector had to tread carefully in his dealings with those with money and influence as he couldn't be sure where their tentacles extended to. Being a meticulous man who in his spare time collected historical Italian stamps, Jordi Bruno was used to looking for the finer details.

He would have to buy a nice bunch of flowers for Ella on his way home.

Thursday 16 February – 8.05 a.m.

That morning, Inspector Bruno sat in his office and pondered Secretary Orazio Mancetti's attempt to intimidate him.

How much did Darius Celestini really know about the body? Celestini didn't seem to know what had been hidden in the ceiling though, just because whatever had lain there had been untouched until the maintenance man started his impromptu building work.

Inspector Bruno had asked Ella to keep a discreet eye on anything at the Comune that might be useful to his enquiries but also told her to be very careful.

Was Ella's phone tapped, he considered?

His even?

What lengths did some of those in power go to, to preserve the status quo?

A knock sounded at his office door.

Detective Sergeant Amanda Chilabon was standing there smiling while holding an A4 beige file. 'The file from the regional land registry archives as requested sir,' she reported. 'Darius Celestini owns the Palazzo Gran Sasso and there is a deed of purchase from the 1960's. It is not clear however who the seller was. One document mentions the Italian royal family overthrown in 1945. Some of the documents are missing.'

'Let me have a look Amanda,' Bruno asked, interest piqued, as she gave him the file.

Chilabon was rapidly becoming an important asset to the department with her quiet determination and sheer professionalism, as Bruno had never tired telling her.

'Interesting,' he mused aloud, after scanning the first few pages and sitting back in his chair. 'Right Amanda, we will try a two-pronged attack. I want an official search of the land ownership archives in the Comune, if they still exist. Find out everything you can about the Palazzo Gran Sasso. Owners, tenants and in particular, any other evidence when the Celestini family got involved. I will try my own unofficial source too.'

'Yes, sir,' Chilabon nodded as Bruno motioned her to sit down on one of the chairs by his desk. She was aware of his 'unofficial source at the Comune – his girlfriend Ella.

Bruno picked up his phone and dialled the station's support unit. 'Constable Castello? Bring me a large-scale map of the local area please?'

'Why do you think a body was hidden in the basement of the Palazzo Gran Sasso Amanda?' He then looked up and asked the ceiling a similar question, folding his hands together as he rested them on the desk, waiting for inspiration of some sort to drop into his lap.

Before Chilabon had a chance to offer a suggestion, Constable Castello, an eager uniformed man in his twenties with a serious demeanour knocked and entered the room with a large map in both hands which he proceeded to spread over a wooden table in the middle of Bruno's office.

Thus, Bruno, Chilabon and Castello pored over the map while Bruno picked up the diary retrieved from the ceiling space chronicling military actions the day of the disappearances and roughly pinpointed where Major Edwards had captured the fascist chief Molina. 'Look,' he said. 'This is where the jeep started from,' he said indicating at the Francavilla Comune building overlooking the Adriatic that served as German command post during mid-1944. 'The regimental archive report in the letter from England also corroborated it too. Here is Sulmona,' Bruno then said pointing to a town in the southern part of the region, 'where Molina was to be sent for interrogation. Here also is the Palazzo Gran Sasso in Chieti,' he said as the three separate points forming an unwieldy triangle were scrutinised.

'Palazzo Gran Sasso is off the route they would have taken,' Chilabon observed. 'It's several kilometres to the west. From near Francavilla, where he was captured, it would be easier to take him down the coast to Sulmona avoiding any possible remaining German ambush. Why go inland to Chieti,' Bruno wondered? 'You said Darius Celestini's family bought the palazzo in the 60's?' he said to Chilabon. 'What about Major Molina? He disappeared also. There is no record of him after that day. Palazzo Gran Sasso has nothing to do with all this,' he thought aloud. 'Unless…?'

His musing was brought a halt by a phone call informing Inspector Bruno of the death of Contessa Lanciano.

Friday 17 February – 2.20 p.m.

Ronnie Cabot had been making his way to work along the Corso towards his tram stop to take him to Chieti Scalo when he noticed a black hearse parked on the pavement outside his old palazzo residence. He had never seen one there before or the unusual parking, as previously Tomaso on guard duty outside would have been onto any driver foolhardy enough to park in an unauthorised place. Now he was gone, people parked where they could even those connected with the transporting of the dead, apparently.

Before he could ponder further, a man dressed in black came out of the main entrance and unfolded a stretcher from the back of the car and what seemed like a body bag, ready to go back into the palazzo.

Cabot who had known the building and some of the people in it, went over and to find out more.

'Excuse me,' he said trying to sound as confident as possible with his fragile Italian. 'I used to live here and I am sorry one of my neighbours has died. May I ask who?' he asked as breezily as possible though not hiding his expectation of an answer.

Luckily, the man in black he had accosted realised Ronnie was a foreigner and not likely to have any underlying motive, turned and faced him.'

'Contessa di Lanciano was found dead in her chair,' he said. 'Did you know her?'

'Yes. She was my neighbour. How did she die?' he asked, mouth dropping open.

'Scared to death if you ask me.'

'What?' Ronnie could scarcely believe what he was hearing.

He went and sat on a low boundary wall behind him as he absorbed the shocking news; a terrible thought was creeping over him.

'Was the supernatural visitor he had encountered involved?'
'Why the Contessa?'

*

At roughly the same time, Inspector Bruno and DS Chilabon stood in the late Contessa's living room while a couple of forensic technicians dressed in white suits were checking for any useful fingerprints or DNA on the wooden door frames or the furniture.

The Contessa's body lay hard against the back of the chair, head back with her eyes wide open, her mouth partly filled by her left fist. She was surrounded by clutter of furniture and piled up books where she had lately entertained Ronnie Cabot.

There was no sign of a murder weapon. Suicide? Had she taken something? On the evidence of her face whatever she had experienced or possibly ingested seemed to have brought upon her death. A puzzle.

'No witnesses, I'll bet,' Bruno, his enthusiasm at a quick solution to the case sinking, asked the Carabinieri Officer making notes on his iPad.

'No one so far, sir,' he replied. 'The pathologist,' who had momentarily popped out to his car, 'said time of death was late last night, maybe midnight – ish.'

'I see,' Bruno replied, not seeing really as he is frowning, looked around the location of the body. Then his gaze shifted to the piles of old newspapers and magazines. Could they have been used to bludgeon her? 'It's like she was sat in her chair sir when whoever attacked her,' Chilbon ventured. 'She must have let the attacker in as there's no sign of a forced entry.'

'No obvious bruises on her either Amanda,' he pondered, pursing his lips.

'Strange for a murder victim. Also no murder weapon as far as we can determine?' the forensic technician added.

'Unless the murderer took whatever he used to kill her with him,' Chilabon speculated. 'But what *sort* of weapon are we talking about that leaves no obvious mark on the victim?'

'It's a bit of a mystery sir,' the police constable ventured to Chilabon and Bruno as they watched a forensic technician superficially examine the Contessa for any signs of a struggle. 'Can't fix on the murder weapon and nothing seems to be missing from the kitchen like knives or anything but because it's so cluttered, it's hard to be sure.'

Finally, going out of the apartment to leave the forensic team to process the scene, the inspector scrutinised two apartment front doors both painted red at the other end of the corridor.

Both were emphatically closed.

'No CCTV anywhere,' he sighed aloud to Chilabon, looking vaguely around.

A chill wind then blew across them out of nowhere, forcing the detectives to pull their coats tighter around themselves and leave as quickly as possible.

A permanently open car park meant there was no one on duty there either so potential witnesses to the murderer entering or exiting the palazzo would be hard to track down unless the police made an appeal in the media.

'Constable?' Jordi Bruno called the officer in the victim's apartment on his police mobile.

'I want all doors knocked on, starting with the victim's floor. See if anyone saw anything.'

*

Signor Orazio Mancetti the party secretary sighed loudly when being informed of Ella Frantoni's call to Inspector Bruno informing him of Darius' unusual visit to the Comune. 'Well Signora Ceresa, let's see what she does next. Check any other outside line she uses okay? Without letting her know we know about her calling the cops.'

This meddling woman was getting to be a nuisance.

*

Sitting in his office, Jordi Bruno pondered his next move with a double espresso from the white jacketed in-house waiter whose modest salary the whole police station subsidised.

He had no obvious leads in the Contessa's death and seemingly no evidence from the crime scene to identify a suspect. The frozen expression on her face unnerved him and he doubted door knocking would elicit much more evidence as neither apartment opposite had a window facing the corridor the visitor would have used arriving and departing the murder scene unless they had shimmied down a rope from the roof, he thought with a bitter chuckle.

His mind drifted back to the conversation he had had DS Chilabon earlier in the day when his train of thought regarding the motive for hiding a body in a building well away from where the initial events of the military transportation had unfolded. He sat back in his chair, arms folded as he tried to put himself into the minds of the suspected murderer of anti-fascist soldier Margaretta and presumably her male colleague Testaladi. 'I've

98

overpowered the two soldiers guarding me,' he related out loud. 'I have forced them then to do as I say with the concealed pistol I am carrying. There is war and chaos everywhere with the battle for control of Pescara raging only a few miles north. Where do I go to make a quick getaway to?'

A pause while traffic hummed in the background and a few shouts from Primary school nearby drifted in Bruno's open window.

A slow smile then crept around the sides of his mouth as they both rose with one accord.

'To a place I know, particularly the fifth-floor apartment.'

*

6.16 p.m.
It had gone six o'clock and most of the Comune staff had gone home.

Ella Frantoni needed to discreetly get into the archived files in its cavernous basement that chronicled most property purchases in the city and the Palazzo Gran Sasso in particular, going back many decades. She was looking for any reference to the Celestini or the Molina families in these property purchases but Jordi Bruno warned her to tread carefully. Darius Celestini or his local well-connected friends mustn't know either Bruno or his mole in the Comune were sifting through any paper trail, however ancient.

Deciding that the coast was clear so late in the working day, she left her desk on the top floor of the enormous Comune building and made her way down the main stairway and past the night security guards who lounged in armchairs in the darkened reception area. Using the pretext that she was working late and returning files to the basement for storage she waved to them and

99

descended the narrow marble stairs to the basement after switching on the strip lights to provide illumination.

Using the keypad she keyed in the code and went into the storage area.

Tall dark wooden shelves, filled to almost overflowing with files and dusty documents filled the entire vast floor space.

Where to start?

She found a roughly alphabetical sequence for everything stored and eventually after much traipsing up and down gloomy dusty aisles she found the files on Palazzo Gran Sasso.

What she found surprised her.

An almost empty box file.

Where were the deeds of purchase?

Details of sales and previous owners?

Shining her small powerful torch on the contents, all Ella found were old inventories of building works dating back years and antique lists of tenants in the various apartments. Any documents signed were invariably illegible or by the person drawing up the document.

She stopped and drew breath sadly.

There was nothing here that would help Jordi Bruno in his investigation.

The relevant documents on the palazzo had been removed.

She guessed by whom.

Ella decided to leave it for now and get back to her office and tidy up before the security guards got suspicious of her loitering in the basement.

However, what she didn't know, what nobody outside the Christian Liberal Party's top executives, numbered on two fingers knew, was that Ella's foray into the archives hadn't gone unnoticed.

Signor Orazio Mancetti, without informing the mayor,

municipality or anyone else using the Comune, had installed a very small security camera over the door to the basement. It was hidden between two cobwebby bricks and provided a sideways image of anyone going past. The image was then sent by a secretly installed WIFI router to the party secretary's laptop.

A little beep on his computer informed him that the basement had been accessed out of hours.

His eyes widened when he realised who it was.

Darius Celestini needed to know.

Saturday 18 February – Ten a.m.

The phone rang several times before Ronnie Cabot gave up.

This was the second time he had tried to call Anna in a couple of days.

They had planned to meet at Caffe Vittorio on the Saturday night, not for a date as such but both seemed to feel they had things in common and liked each other's company. For her just to not answer seemed strange.

He didn't have her address so for now, he decided to leave it for a couple of days before trying again.

Outside the snow fell in gentle white feathery tufts.

The small cafe downstairs from his apartment in the piazza which sold hot drinks and croissants was the furthest he would venture for now.

*

The two men met at the local Chieti Masonic lodge.

It was the safest place to meet away from prying eyes and ears.

They didn't go into the lodge itself, a large 1970's construction of steel and glass with an extensive balcony with open views of the Apennine mountains in the distance.

'She's been snooping around in the basement and probably in touch with the police again,' the squat bearded man said through his open window in a calm measured voice.

'Bloody woman, she's trying to tie me in with the murder victims and maybe take my business away! What can I do?' he asked pursing his lips.

'We could sack her, make up some reason but it won't be easy. Labour laws grind slowly in this country as you know,' the first man said shrugging.

'If she's not careful the laws are going to grind bloody sight faster than she could ever realise!' the other man said before starting to drive away. 'Keep me informed,' he shouted out of his window as his Mercedes scrunched up the gravel as it exited the car park.

*

12.25 p.m.
On Saturday lunchtime, Mauro Andretti, Ronnie's student from the Commune, picked him up in his yellow *cinquecento* from outside his new apartment next to the old Roman amphitheatre in down town Chieti.

He was taking Ronnie to his house-warming dinner at his new flat in Citta Sant' Angelo, a smaller version of Chieti on a hill to the north that could be seen from Cabot's previous apartment.

Like Chieti, Citta Sant' Angelo's main street threaded its way along the ridge of the hill, along which colourful medieval and modern buildings stood cheek by jowl, fighting for who had the best views or the shadiest gardens. Mauro's newly renovated flat in a palazzo, was similar to Ronnie's first apartment though much smaller, and just off the town centre next to the Chiesa di San Giovanni, a beautiful bright medieval church with a high bell tower offering bucolic views across the southern Abruzzese hills.

'At least, you'll know when Mass starts!' Ronnie said laughing at Mauro, as they both stood on Mauro's first floor balcony, cold beers in hand.

'I am an atheist, don't forget,' Mauro said which took Ronnie somewhat aback. Mauro noticed Ronnie's raised eyebrows. 'Ah ha, you think all Italians are how you say *devout?*' No, my friend,' he continued. 'Most people I know especially the educated are *maybe* believers?'

'*Agnostics*' Ronnie replied.

'Precisely,' he said. 'People like me think the Catholic church has done enough to keep the people ignorant. After the war the church was accused of supporting the German occupation so now in these modern times I think people want to take control of their own destiny. Not priests,' he said with an air that sounded to Ronnie that there was still an underpinning of resentment to this segment of society that had not abated in the long years since 1945.

Ronnie could do no more than listen attentively. The Anglican church from his own country had been accused of many things over the years from child abuse to supporting slavery but it had never colluded in a foreign occupation so he, as a foreigner, had to defer to Mauro's point of view.

Other fellow invited students from the Comune joined Ronnie and Mauro on the balcony hearing their conversation and affirmed Mauro's scepticism of religious authority. Cabot wanted to change the subject and mention his love of Roman archaeology, in particular, ask to visit the bathhouse ruins in the old city centre at some point. He could also no more than affirm how Italians ran their society was really their business. He was an outsider and a guest of the Italians he had met and communed with since his arrival six months ago.

'Let me show you my collection,' Mauro whispered, almost conspiratorially as friends of his started to leave and go home.

Ronnie's eyebrows rose.

What was Mauro talking about?

Mauro took Ronnie to a room at the end of his apartment corridor and there on a wooden table at least six feet long was his model soldier collection comprising, Mauro said, the Italian army in a North African 1942 setting and the opposing forces of the British Eighth army.

'Wow!' Ronnie was impressed, as much by the model palm trees and rustic buildings as much as the soldiers.

Even more so, as he hadn't told anyone of his own Napoleonic model soldier collection in boxes in England. 'I like your attention to detail,' he continued as he studied the mock up desert terrain and the well painted soldiers and equipment.

'You see Ron,' Mauro continued, taking off his glasses and picking up a metal Italian officer figure off the table, Italy didn't want to fight the British Empire in 1939. It was that bastard Hitler who forced *Il Duce* to fight with him. Our leader was more interested in North Africa and the Middle East.'

Cabot didn't like to mention that wherever the Italian army had been ordered to fight by their dictator or the Germans, they would have inevitably come into contact with the British Empire.

After promising to bring Ronnie over for a future war game, Mauro's parents called them both to the kitchen where the clean-up from the dinner had started. They had prepared so much food for the occasion that Mauro's smiling parents presented Ronnie with, via Mauro's translation, a large *'doggy bag'* to take home, after assuring everyone present that it had nothing to do with dogs and no, he didn't know why it was called that? He had drunk so much local wine that he fell asleep in the taxi Mauro provided for Cabot to get home.

Sunday 19 February – 7.38 p.m.

Inspector Bruno went to work via the Palazzo Gran Sasso early on Sunday morning in a pensive mood.

It was well documented that a man identified after the war by local residents as Major Molina, had indeed shot at people from the fifth floor of the Palazzo Gran Sasso during the German occupation, but was there any evidence left that this was why the body of one of his captors was found there? Evidence of the bullet recovered from the body behind the boiler pointed to someone armed with a Luger murdered Margaretta. Lugers were only issued to officers so was the murderer Molina? As an officer he would have been issued with one, so it seemed. If he had murdered Margaretta, where was the other soldier? Buried somewhere in the vicinity? It was also possible that someone had picked up the Luger in those chaotic days of 1944 and done the deed, for whatever reason, being entirely unrelated to the Major's disappearance.

Ella's text telling him that the municipal archives concerning the sale or purchase of Palazzo Gran Sasso were missing, puzzled him. They must have existed at one time. Was Signor Orazio Mancetti or someone in the party covering up for Darius Celestini? If so how else could Jordi Bruno move the case forward?

Inspector Bruno walked up and down the Gran Sasso stairs, looking around like a tourist on a guided tour but now he was self-guiding alone and trying to learn what he could.

Or was he alone?

Someone, evidently elderly and carrying a mop was blocking the top of the last set of stairs that led to the street.

He walked towards her.

She stood impassively leaning on her mop but something told him she wanted to help him.

The Inspector towered over the old lady dressed in her old full length faded grey coat that she probably had worn for years. Her hair was tied back in a tight knot under an equally faded head scarf.

'Hello Signora,' he ventured, 'did you see anything suspicious last Thursday night?' he asked in dialect and opening his police warrant card though probably she couldn't see it.

A pause.

The two parties scrutinised each other; one more warily than the other.

'Well?'

'Maybe son,' she drawled, folding her arms as she looked for a cigarette that obviously didn't exist.

Bruno quickly found one for her from his coat pocket and lit it.

After introducing himself again as a police inspector, an extended dialogue in broadest Abruzzese dialect followed which even Bruno struggled to make sense of.

She, Violetta Crimosa she introduced herself as, had apparently seen a figure in a dark coat from the window of her garret flat she pointed to, which Bruno had previously dismissed as being empty. The figure had gone into the Contessa's flat, she said but hadn't seen it come out. Well, the inspector had found a witness though he wasn't sure how much use she was. She wasn't keen on going to the police station to provide a statement for a start.

Sitting down later in his leather chair and already loosening the collar of the crisp white shirt he was wearing, Jordi Bruno ordered an espresso from the police station waiter as he picked up the phone and switched on his laptop which he normally kept hidden away from prying eyes in a pull-out counter under the desk.

'Amanda, come in here please?'

DS Chilabon opened the office door and walked in, standing nearly to attention at his desk.

'Send a police artist over to the Palazzo Gran Sasso that speaks dialect. The old cleaner may have seen the back of our killer and will help produce a drawing if anyone can understand what she says.'

'Yes, sir.'

'Then come back here please,' Bruno continued. 'By the way, have you managed to unearth any Palazzo Gran Sasso documents yet?'

'No, sir,' Chilabon admitted, transferring her weight from one leg to another. 'I put in request with the public relations department and…'

'Okay, keep trying,' Bruno interrupted her. 'My source though established that the documents we are interested in are gone from the archive. We aren't giving up though,' he continued, pounding his right fist on the desk which was supposed to convince DS Sergeant Davide as he turned to read his email from the archive clerk in Pescara.

He became so absorbed in it and particularly the attachment sent to him that he had no idea if Amanda Chilabon was still in the room. She could have stripped off (which was hundred per cent unlikely anyway) and he wouldn't have noticed.

Actually DS Chilabon had temporarily exited the room, amused by her boss's sabre rattling, returning a minute or so later along with the coffee attendant who had bought double espressos for her and Bruno as he indicated for her to pull up a chair to his desk.

'Who's that do you think?' Bruno asked turning his laptop round facing Chilabon.

She could see a faded black and white passport type photograph of a man in a wartime military uniform with a military officer's hat.

DS Chilabon put on her reading glasses and then removed them as quickly before looking slowly up at her boss. 'It looks like Signor Celestini,' she replied. 'But it can't be, can it? He wasn't born then.'

'His father was,' Bruno replied, as Major Molina's face stared back at them.

Monday 20 February – Seven Thirty a.m.

Inspector Bruno had to wait until the following morning for the developments in the case as he sat down in his office chair, scanned post lying on his desk and switched on his computer.

DS Chilabon knocked and then came into the office with a man in a scruffy jacket and long hair. A *fashionista* he was not, though he had one skill Bruno valued.

He was the police artist and his picture was ready, Chilabon informed the inspector. Did he wish to see it?

'Immediately,' Bruno replied.

He then picked up the phone to call front desk.

'Station Sergeant Degrelli, send a car to pick up Ronnie Cabot from his apartment and bring him over. Wake him up if necessary, okay?

'Yes, sir,' Degrelli would organise a patrol car.

*

As Ronnie hadn't got through to Inspector Bruno when he had tried to call him a week or so earlier, Bruno sent the police car to Cabot's old address. A call had to then be made on Cabot's mobile to locate him and bring him finally to the police station.

*

An hour or so later, after Bruno finally tracked Ronnie down to his new address, he was ensconced in the policeman's office after hastily finishing his breakfast at an hour earlier than he normally did. The Carabinieri officer who knocked on Cabot's door had told him the inspector needed to talk to him as soon as possible at the station.

The artist's pencilled picture was laid on Bruno's desk.

'Does the profile look familiar Signor Cabot?' he asked.

Ronnie was confused and his shoulders dropped.

'What's the matter? Don't you recognise her?' Bruno asked noticing his discomfort. 'My artist sat with the signora and had to endure a long story about her life and the shortcomings of her job. And her landlord!

'Yes, I recognise her but it's not like you think. I tried to call you before after what I saw,' Cabot replied. 'I only saw her from the front,' Cabot continued scrutinising the heavy features of the flowing dark hair, solid shoulders and an almost military straight-backed posture.

'Who?' Bruno asked.

'The girl I dreamed about.

The girl who appeared in my bedroom.

This is I wanted to tell you about but you weren't there when I called.'

'What the hell?' Bruno looked frowning into Ronnie's face as they both stood leaning over the picture. 'D'you realise what you are saying to me Signor Cabot? A ghost went into the Contessa's apartment and frightened the old soul to death?'

Ronnie sighed loudly and shrugged his shoulders. 'I know it sounds crazy inspector but I saw the undertaker who brought her body out from her apartment. I told him I had been her neighbour and then he told me about the shock all over her face when they found her,' Cabot replied awkwardly, his paranormal encounter with the murdered woman no longer a safe secret.

'Right, I see,' Jordi Bruno said slowly, trying to see if Cabot

111

was really helping as he picked up the artist's impression and gave it to DS Chilabon to pin up on the evidence wall in the next room. He then picked up the phone to his Station Sergeant. 'The next part of the plan.'

*

There was a fair amount of curtain twitching among the well-heeled residents of Palazzo Gran Sasso as two teams of Carabinieri armed with what seemed like metal detectors slowly made their way around the ground floor, one sweeping the long-handled machine out ahead of them and the other monitoring results on headphones and iPad.

'Police business,' was the oft quoted response when residents parking or generally coming and going from the building button-holed the busy constables, asking their business. Though a fierce wind blew along the corridors and stairways, the officers in their greatcoats made steady progress as they covered the whole floor surface area, grid by grid.

After an hour or so, the two groups of officers retired to the comparative warmth of their vehicles parked up on the pavement. Notes were compared and the iPad results cross-examined.

Nothing suspicious was indicated in any of the floor areas. Nothing that looked like a buried anomaly or a floor disturbance in any way.

Inspector Bruno was not happy to hear this negative outcome but finished his phone call with his officers with the satisfaction that it was one action he could cross off in the search for a body. The cold constables were allowed to return to base.

Just then he got a call from Constable Castello who was wrapping up his search of the Contessa's apartment.

'I've found something interesting,' the constable said curbing his excitement until his boss had officially congratulated him for some excellent police work.

'Bring it over to me constable straight away.'

*

<u>7.20 p.m.</u>
Signor Darius Celestini, always somewhat over-organised and permanently on the move with one project or another was strangely still in his office.

His hunch that Tomaso had somehow smuggled home items he had found in the ceiling had so unnerved him that he used his informal local connections again including a sympathetic police officer for some discreet information.

Three addresses, two within half an hour of the Corso Marrucino that may help him resolve his suspicion were duly texted to him, scribbled on a notepad and stored in the wallet he always carried in his coat pocket.

He also studied information passed on to him by his contact at the Comune, Signora Michele Ceresa.

Tomaso Scilaci's address could be investigated. Though the ex-caretaker's eyesight wasn't so good, he could have taken home something he had found but getting into his apartment would be difficult as his elderly parents' lived there. The second address was a remote location in a valley not far from town but the third was the most promising. The resident there was quite capable of putting two and two together and running to the police with any conclusions.

Darius pondered what to do, sitting still in his chair and staring at the bookcase opposite as his mind worked through various possibilities of future actions to protect himself and his businesses.

Then, abruptly he got up and left his office.

He went out to his car parked in the closed car park at the back of the institute. Punching the relevant address into his satnav, he set off for Pescara in his streamlined black Jaguar.

*

'It's definitely him,' Jordi Bruno agreed, as he studied the black and white photograph in a faded gold leaf frame Constable Castello was holding next to Bruno's desk. The inspector then took out a magnifying glass from a desk drawer for a closer inspection. 'Well done, Castello.'

There was Major Molina in a warm embrace with a well-dressed younger version of the late Contessa, taken probably during the war as he was in a uniform and she was wearing 1940's fashions.

'I found it in one of the drawers stuffed with old papers, sir,' Castello said triumphantly beaming back at his boss.

Inspector Bruno next took out a passport sized photo of a man Constable Castello didn't know and laid it next to the Major's photo.

'What do you see?' Bruno asked.

'The Major and someone who looks like the Major,' replied Castello casually. 'Wow!' he suddenly realised the implications of what he as seeing. 'Who is this then?'

'A prominent local businessman and English language school owner, Darius Celestini.'

Inspector Bruno privately wondered whether any other conclusions could be drawn.

Tuesday 21 February – Eight a.m.

Meantime, Darius had been busy.

His safe in his small Termoli sea-side apartment was no longer secure he reckoned for the important documents he had inherited from his father.

If the police got a search warrant for his villa, they would start poking around so deciding that he should move his papers away from prying eyes, he put a full leather briefcase into his car in the early hours and drove over to the Comune, parking in the underground private car park which membership of the Christian Liberal Party had given him privileged access to.

Looking nervously around, a bit unnecessary in a secure car park and in theory inaccessible to the general public, he made his way to a receptionist on duty at the Comune front desk.

'This must be given to party secretary Mancetti immediately,' he said grim-faced, trying not to betray his shaking hand.

'Certainly signor,' the smartly dressed secretary replied, putting it in her desk at the back of the office and locking it.

Darius, satisfied his possessions were safe now, turned and left.

Because it wasn't even eight o'clock in the morning yet, when most party workers clocked on, the stylishly dressed secretary was the only person on duty.

She knew she had to call her boyfriend as soon as the visitor had gone.

Picking up the phone she dialled an ex-directory home landline.

'Jordi,' she said in a hushed tone as he picked up the phone. 'It's me. Signor Celestini has just left a bag stuffed with documents at party HQ. What shall I do?'

'Really?' he tried to restrain his excitement. 'Quick, try and see what's inside.'

Bruno had to think quickly.

A court order at this hour would be problematic and maybe alert Mancetti though this may be the only opportunity of stealing a march on Celestini and Mancetti's attempt to thwart his investigation.

Bruno and particularly his mole had to be circumspect.

'Check out any documents concerning the Palazzo Gran Sasso. Try and photocopy them but be careful darling. See you after work okay?' he said putting down the receiver immediately. He didn't know if the anyone could trace a call made from within the building, even to a name withheld number.

They could.

*

Anna sat at her study table in the student halls of residence, her books open in front of her. She needed to revise for an upcoming exam but after an hour or so she had had enough and decided to go over to the student canteen.

Putting on her thick winter coat and hat, she quietly let herself out of the room and made her way to the stairs. She wanted to call Ronnie as a catch up and maybe meet up later.

Darius Celestini, used a paid contact at the prestigious G. D'Annunzio university in Pescara, as a result of having organised student accommodation in the past, to find Anna's residence block number and room number from reception. After going back to lock his car parked on the on Via Fonte Romana, he made his way across the sprawling campus to one corner. Scrutinising the piece of paper in the winter gloom, he saw the relevant garish sixties residential block and the glass double doors that offered access.

Climbing up the stairs from the draughty hallway he casually passed a young woman wrapped up against the winter cold going in the opposite direction.

He didn't have a description of the female student who resided in the room he was interested in, having never met her.

However, Anna knew what *he* looked like so kept walking, legs wobbling slightly and unnerved by what his motives might be in trying to find her. Knowing the dog tags were still known about only by herself and her uncle and momentarily afraid of leaving the evidence for him to find, she momentarily lingered at the bottom of the stairs in the hallway.

Should she go back and confront him? Not advisable with most people out of the building. She couldn't wait there. He might come back at any time, recognise her from the stairs and guess it was her he was looking for.

She continued out of the door and over to the canteen where she decided to wait.

It was a pity she couldn't call the police.

*

Deciding that a locked student residence door wasn't going to stop him, Darius took out a special key that gained access to most rooms.

117

Years of having to break into properties of his for reasons including non-payment of rent or flight of the tenants, had taught him simple skills that now served his purpose. He needed to know if Tomaso's niece had anything of his from the hidden ceiling cavity, so having quickly gained access Celestini was confronted with a small dark student room. Putting a bedside light on, he took in a single bed and a wardrobe along with a study desk and chair; sparse but tidy enough he concluded. His mind raced now.

Where to look?

He didn't have much time.

The desk had a locked drawer.

Taking the special key out again he swiftly jemmied the drawer open and saw a little beige felt bag.

Opening it quickly, he poured the metallic contents onto his outstretched hand and then sat back on the bed in a state of shock, an unusual emotion for him, it had to be said.

He had never seen these dog tags before.

He had over the years speculated that such things might exist but had been content to do nothing, confident that if they were indeed secreted somewhere in the Palazzo Gran Sasso, they were unlikely to see the light of day unless the whole place burned down!

Until the girl's stupid uncle took a crowbar to the ceiling.

Celestini pulled himself together quickly.

He got up and let himself out as quietly as possible and scurried down the first-floor corridor and the stairs out of the apartment block.

Examining the dog tags in his car his heart sank. The authorities were probably going to find out the names of the two missing militia and by extension, how he Darius Celestini may fit into the mystery.

He sighed.

A call came through on his mobile.

'I got your case but I think it has been tampered with,' the man on the other end of the line informed him.

'How do you know?' Celestini asked.

'Ella Frantoni was the only person on duty when you handed it in. She would have had plenty of time to have a look at its contents.'

'Dam!' Celestini shouted down the phone. 'I didn't know it was *her* at reception at that time of the morning! Of all the people I could have handed it to.'

'Well, I don't know what she has copied but I *will* find an excuse to get rid of her,' the caller assured him.

A pause on the line.

'What kind of car does she drive?' Celestini enquired.

*

An hour or so later, when Anna returned to her flat and checked the study desk drawer, she realised what Darius had been after.

The beige bag was empty.

She immediately called her uncle.

At least she had photographed the incriminating objects on her mobile phone.

*

Three thirty p.m.

Inspector Giordano Bruno had just got off his mobile after leaving a message on Ella Frantoni's voice mail. It was, he had decided, getting too risky for her to pass on any more information from the Comune so she should just stop and preferably, take a holiday.

Scarcely was the phone down when Station Sergeant

Degrelli was on the line.

'I've just had that caretaker from Palazzo Gran Sasso on the phone telling me about some dog tags he 'found' during his poke about in Signor Cabot's apartment ceiling.'

'What?' Bruno shouted as he almost collapsed into his leather chair. 'Where *are* these tags sergeant?'

'He says they were stolen from his niece's room at Pescara university,' Degrelli said almost sheepishly down the phone.

'*Niece's room*!' Bruno couldn't contain his cool calm exterior any longer. 'What the hell were they doing there?

'No idea. He did say his niece saw who stole them.

She did photograph them,' Degrelli said lamely.

The inspector had had enough of this.

'Send two uniforms with a car and get this idiot's statement now. If this Scilaci gets stroppy or uncooperative they can arrest him and find her too. I'll do them both for burglary! Also sergeant, dispatch two constables round to Signor Celestini's school and two to his villa in Termoli. I want him here now whatever he's doing!'

'Yes, sir.'

Bruno reached into a drawer and took out the battered black leather action diary retrieved from the ceiling cavity.

He went over to a locked cabinet in the corner of the office.

Unlocking it he took out a small bottle and glass and poured a generous measure as he sat on the radiator next to a side window. He told himself he deserved a quick pick-me-up before he had to deal with Signor Tomaso Scilaci and whoever else was tagging along.

*

Early Evening

Ella Frantoni got into her red Skoda Felicia, having finished work at the Comune and waved her plastic ID card at the car park barrier which then lifted up and let her out.

Snaking round the steep roads down the hill from Chieti's ancient heart to the plain below through the southern suburb of Frasoli she joined the main road to Bucchianico, on Chieti's south east skyline. The iPhone with which she had quickly photographed a selection of Darius Celestini's property documents was safe in her handbag; she would forward them to her boyfriend as soon as she was home.

Living alone in a luxury flat just off the small town's historic centre, known as the centre of fine dining, she looked forward to seeing her partner who was coming to her place over later on.

What she hadn't spotted in the commuter traffic was a dark blue Volvo with tinted glass that had started shadowing her movements. Stuck at Frasoli's interminable traffic lights, Ella switched on her car radio and wound down the window. The evening was drawing in and it looked like snow.

The lights eventually changed and Ella wound up her window again. Two streams of traffic made their way along the Strada Delle Pace in the gathering gloom. Staying in the slower lane in this bad weather, she preferred to let faster cars overtake her.

Now, the Volvo had manoeuvred into a position behind Ella's Skoda as the road started to veer round to the left avoiding a drop on the opposite side.

In the gloom, Ella, looking in her rear mirror thought nothing of the dark car following her now. As soon as she got in, she would have a quick shower, call her parents and then get changed before meeting Jordi later. Then she would…

'Dammit,' she exclaimed as her mobile phone slipped out of its cradle above the central dashboard and clattered into the front passenger seat foot well.

She hadn't securely attached it.

The traffic seemed flowing steadily enough for her to slip off her seatbelt and reach down to grab it from off the passenger seat black rubber foot mat.

Momentarily gazing down in the gloom to snatch it with her right hand, almost got it…

Crash!

Ella's car lurched violently forward.

Her Skoda had been rammed in the rear, temporarily throwing her against the steering wheel, as the car swerved under the weight of the impact.

Flailing around with her arms in the driver's seat, she tried to regain control but the car had gone too far to the verge for the tyres to respond to her frantic attempt to steer.

For a second her car raced along the road, hard against the kerb before the whole vehicle lifted off and flipped over as it careered down the slope, surrounding cars slamming on their brakes and swerving as they tried to avoid the stricken car.

The accident perpetrator driving the Volvo drove on, showing no regard for other people's safety, aggressively changing lanes and then sped up, escaping down a nearby side road and into the dark.

An off-duty policeman making his way home a few cars behind Ella, saw the dark coloured Volvo up close briefly and was able to later confirm that it had no number plate.

Meanwhile, Ella's car had careered to the bottom of a slope enveloped in a basket of several trees and extensive bracken, its lights on and engine running.

Up above on the main road cars screeched and swerved in an attempt to avoid the debris littering the road after the rammed car had lurched off the carriage way down the snowy damp verge.

*

Ronnie Cabot arrived home around ten p.m. after getting off the tram from Chieti Scalo after his evening teaching adults English. Anna had sent him a text asking him when he would be home so she could meet him at his flat at the little piazza. This excited him as well as worried him. What did she want so late? A taxi back to her student accommodation in Pescara would be costly at this time of night.

Walking up to his building, he saw her wrapped up against the night waiting by his first-floor front door. She looked pretty he thought though this observation was mixed with tiredness after an afternoon and evening on his feet. He just wanted to get in, have a tea and sit down with his laptop.

'Haven't heard from you for a while,' he said trying not to sound too annoyed at her recent reticence towards him.

'Sorry,' she said putting her hands deep in her winter coat pockets. 'I have been busy,' she said awkwardly telling him nothing. Then, 'Can I come in? She asked smiling looking at floor.

'Okay sure,' Ronnie said walking past her and opening his apartment door. He switched on the lights to drive away the darkness and put his coat and satchel on the sofa.

She took her coat off and sat down.

At length with beers in their hands instead of tea with the heating on, Anna continued, sighing and frowning as she spoke. 'I am sorry what my uncle did when he broke into your old flat.

123

He made a hole in the ceiling and found some items that dated back to the war but didn't want to tell the police at the beginning because he doesn't trust them. He found dog tags that seemed to prove the identity of two soldiers escorting the Major. If his aunt was buried in the palazzo building he reckons the other soldier is too.'

'He's got to be careful your uncle,' Ronnie replied after listening to her tale. 'and so have you. Darius is well connected especially with the Comune.'

Anna, deliberately changing the subject, noticed Ronnie's red and white football calendar on the wall.

'Is that your team Ronnie?' she asked.

'Yep,' he answered smiling.

'How do you pronounce it?' she continued as she furrowed her alluring dark eyebrows, concentrated on the three-syllable word. 'Middle-s-broug? Bug?'

'*Middlesbrough!*' Ronnie said emphatically with a smile. 'That's where I was born!'

'Middles – what?' Anna answered laughing. 'Why can't you English wrote words that you can pronounce – *like us Italians!*'

'Because a thousand years ago my dear,' Ronnie replied chuckling, 'my bleedin' ancestors *did* pronounce all the letters! It's just we've just moved on a bit in the interim but loads of our words haven't and my home town is one of them! What about you living in *Chieti?*' Ronnie added laughing. 'I thought CHIETI rhymed with cheese!'

*

The laughter decreased into small-talk for some time as they gradually became less awkward towards each other. Sitting next

124

to each other and beers finished, Cabot thought he should make a move but was reluctant to make it towards Anna.

Did she expect him to?

Or a move just telling her he was off to bed?

He erred on the side of least resistance as he got up to leave.

'You can have the sofa, I'm off to my scratcher now,' he said mock jovially, half-wanting to see her reaction to some real slang she wouldn't learn on a university language course!

'Scratcher?' she asked smiling wearily. What more weird words was she learning about this absurd language that had conquered the world?

'Yes, that's what we called it when we were students because…you *scratch* there,' Ronnie smiled back, mimicking the activity and picking up a large woollen blanket from a wardrobe in the hall to give her.

'Okay,' she replied.

Too tired for now, he excused himself to the bathroom before going to bed.

Anna, meanwhile, peeped into his large bedroom, realising bizarrely, it was larger than the so-called living room.

A large bay window overlooking the piazza and lacking any curtains was several feet off the ground. Views of surrounding buildings were visible from floor level without any possibility of Ronnie being overlooked.

In the corner under several white painted shelves was a large single bed, unmade with an empty coffee cup and bible on a small, what seemed like an upside-down bucket covered in a white cloth. A study desk with an angle lamp was against the opposite wall with a large faded blue carpet in the middle of the room – an old heavy radiator against the outside wall provided more than adequate heat for the room.

She retreated back to the living room sofa as Ronnie going

the other way, wished her goodnight. She then switched off the living room lamp and lay down with a blanket Ronnie had given her. The sofa was surprisingly comfortable considering it was second hand and showed evidence of a recent deep clean.

Soon, she too was asleep.

Late Evening

Inspector Bruno had been home since around seven after the constables called from Darius' school to say he wasn't there or at his villa at Termoli.

He had decided to leave pursuing Celestini for now.

He would also have a look at Tomaso's statement in the morning.

Meantime, he relaxed, watching TV at home but was mystified why he couldn't get in touch with Ella despite calling her house and her parents' house. Sitting in front of his glass balcony doors at his suburban Francavilla apartment he wondered what had happened to her before he got a call around ten p.m. from the local hospital.

He was out of the door in seconds as he raced to his car.

*

After ditching the Volvo in a quiet unlit lane the man walked gingerly along in the darkness lest he trip over an unsuspecting hole, his greatcoat wrapped tightly around him, gloves on and woollen hat pulled down over his face.

He had done what he had had to do.

No nosey little bitch was going to get in his way and threaten what he had built up, he told himself bitterly.

Presently after doubling back and walking a couple of kilometres along the verge of the main road, he reached the next suburb nearby the Adriatic coast. Finding a taxi rank, he convinced one of the drivers with a wad of cash as he was knocking off to drive him to the coast, making sure his features were concealed as much as possible.

*

Inspector Domenico Drago, was hurriedly briefed by Abruzzo's top policeman Deputy Director Cosimo Nerone on the shocking attack on Frantoni as he sat in the police helicopter heading east from his Rome police station over to Chieti hospital's roof helipad the other side of the Apennines.

Soon after, Jordi Bruno's police car, driven west from Franca' and siren blaring, was screaming to a halt outside Accident and Emergency as Inspector Drago was being apprised by a local Carabinieri unit already parked outside.

A man of similar age to Bruno with short greying hair over his square military type visage, Drago was a man who looked like a leader, demanding loyalty from his subordinates above all else.

In return he would go through fire for them if they needed help negotiating paperwork mountains or inflexible, play-it-safe senior police types higher up the police food chain.

Unlike his colleague Domenico Drago was happily married to Carmella with a brood of five children, the eldest Marco being at police training college. He was loathe to leave Carmella but she, knowing the uncertainties of a policeman's duty took it in her stride as he called with profuse apologies while he was airborne.

This was an emergency Nerone had emphasised to him.

His colleague would be hopelessly compromised trying to investigate the attack on Ella Frantoni, Bruno's girlfriend working discreetly for him at the Comune, gathering intelligence on Darius Celestini's nefarious business dealings, in particular his purchase of the Palazzo Gran Sasso.

Signora Carmella Drago as devout a Catholic as her husband was nevertheless only able to do a certain amount of household tasks during the day without his help.

She was then relieved when her husband had told her he had hired a home help with immediate effect to assist her in feeding and clothing the four younger children ranging from two years to sixteen, the eldest, Marco, being at police college.

*

Soon enough, Drago's bear-like comforting hand was on Bruno's shoulder as they encountered each other in the hospital car park 'Emergency' entrance, bathed in flashing blue and white colours of two police cars.

Bruno had been pacing about the small driveway like a man possessed – the Carabinieri officers keeping him from running into the Emergency entrance.

'What are you doing here inspector?' Jordi Bruno blurted out looking frantically at his friend and then over the police officers' outstretched arms for a doorway that may lead him to Ella. 'What happened? Where is she? No one's telling me.'

'The hospital told me she was in a car accident,' Inspector Drago said facing his friend whose arms, devoid of any strength hung limply now by his side. 'I was alerted by your boss Deputy Nerone and asked to help out. He sent me at top speed by helicopter from Rome to help out half an hour ago.'

'The hospital dialled her most recent number called on her phone and it was mine obviously,' Bruno continued, only half listening to the incoming inspector's explanation for *his* appearance.

Bruno focused on making his way into the hospital in search of the doctors struggling to keep Ella Frantoni alive.

'Wait, wait!' Domenico Drago and two other constables struggled to restrain the frantic inspector as he tried to push past them, his eyes wide with panic. 'Come here and sit down,' Drago said gently leading his friend to a bench inside the emergency area normally reserved for the hospital staff. All around them health workers busied themselves with the steady stream of other accident and emergency admissions from the local area. 'I didn't know you were seeing her,' Drago explained. 'Nerone wants me to investigate the attack for you.'

'Why would you need to know who I'm seeing?' Bruno shouted. Then, 'Sorry Dom, don't know what I am doing? What's happening to me?' Bruno shouted tearfully at his friend as he crumpled down on the white wooden bench.

The accompanying policeman's radio crackled with news.

He passed it to Domenico Drago who went a hue of cold ash.

He looked gravely at Jordi Bruno who stared equally gravely back at him, silent now.

Sitting in his crumpled suit with unkempt hair, Jordi realised the worst.

'She didn't make it Jordi,' Drago said putting his right arm around his friend's shoulders, fighting to keep his emotions in check.

Bruno, overcome with emotion, could do nothing but weep silently, his hands covering his eyes.

'An off-duty copper saw a Volvo with no plates ram her off the road,' Drago continued quietly, looking at the floor. Then turning to his friend, 'We'll find the bastard who did it, don't worry.'

'Oh my God! I pushed her too far!' Jordi Bruno ranted tearfully through his fingers.

'We know your reputation as an honest man sir,' one of the two Carabinieri responded, sitting next to the unashamedly weeping inspector. 'If it was police business you would have done everything by the book sir.'

Drago, meanwhile, wanted to know what his friend meant by saying he had pushed her too far but would leave it for now and along with the other policeman continued a constant radio dialogue with headquarters in Chieti.

'Everyone on the force respects you Inspector Bruno sir, and we will get the bastard,' the Carabinieri officer continued.

Drago was then nudged to take a call on his police phone in his jacket pocket so getting up after patting his friend on the shoulder, Constable Vivante, freshly arrived from the emergency room, sat down where Drago had been.

'The doctor said Ella was alive when they cut her out of the car sir,' the young policeman said quietly. 'But she had lost too much blood and they couldn't resuscitate her when they got her into the trauma room. She was a fighter though sir,' he continued softly.

Drago came back to Bruno and lay a hand again on his shoulder. 'Uniform found an abandoned Volvo not far away with no plates. Forensics are taking it to the pound so they can give it a once over. They have also recovered Ella's car.'

It was time for Drago to lead, as those around him expected him to do and make waves.

Whoever got swamped, tough.

Wednesday 22 February – 8.25 a.m.

The previous night's 'road rage murder,' was the top story on the morning news programme Ronnie was watching on his company supplied TV in his company supplied apartment.

Disbelief and shock grew in his brain that such a thing could happen in such a civilised place as Chieti…

Anna had slipped out at early dawn while he'd been sleeping in his room.

Cabot sat and watched, initially not aware of a connection between the reported road rage murder and the mystery he had been lately involved in. It was only when he was sitting opposite Tiziana's desk at the school in Chieti Scalo that she read back to him the report in the paper mentioning the vague rumour that the crash victim had links to the police department.

'Guesswork Tiziana, it sounds. I wonder what Inspector Bruno's take is on all this?' Ronnie wondered. 'Haven't heard from him for a while.'

*

Station Sergeant Degrelli was in the station early, half-heartedly reviewing a list of motorists caught with major faults on their cars and needing to pay outstanding fines.

His peripheral vision was caught by movement next to Inspector Bruno's open door.

Moving his head slightly to the left he was surprised to see a tall woman in a khaki raincoat noiselessly open Bruno's office door and walk in.

Quick as a flash and to the surprise of the secretary behind him who saw nothing suspicious, he rushed round the two desks between his perch and the chief's office.

Throwing the inspector's door open he was ready to castigate the intruder for somehow getting past his sentry post and take up position in the senior policeman's office, *without a by your leave!*

The room was empty.

Degrelli, taken aback, rather pointlessly looked under Bruno's desk and behind the curtains and peered through the grand double windows.

'She was here,' he turned with a wretched expression as two colleagues stood frowning in the office doorway. 'I saw this woman and now she has gone. It's impossible,' he lamely finished up, flopping in one of Bruno's leather chairs.

Thursday 23 February – 7.47 a.m.

Inspector Jordi Bruno, needless to say, being too affected and compromised by his Ella's murder to be involved in the investigation, was put on official sick-leave by his boss, Deputy Director Cosimo Nerone until further notice.

Inspector Domenico Drago officially took over the Frantoni murder case away from his regular Rome patch.

After ringing wife Carmella to make sure the new home help was duly helping his wife run the house in Rome, Inspector Drago sighed deeply before getting back to work with grim determination.

Acting on Bruno's suggestion, just after seven thirty in the morning, Inspector Drago freshly arrived from his hotel room just off the Corso, sat outside the Palazzo Gran Sasso in a police Land Rover Discovery accompanied by a three Carabinieri officers armed with long spades.

It wasn't clear though how useful shovels would be for the policemen as most of the outside area of the palazzo was either asphalt, paving stones or concrete slabs.

It was also bitterly cold leading all assembled to wonder how long they would have enough energy to battle the elements as well as building materials.

Drago gazed up at the carved stone crest over the palazzo's main entrance.

He knew a bit about heraldry but this was odd; How come a building less than a hundred years old had a family crest with an escutcheon of two lions in two opposite quarters and a two coiled up lengths of rope in the two other corners?

A design which boasted of nobility and glorious ancestry.

Whose noble ancestry?

Perhaps the baroque decoration was an in-joke on the builder's part maybe? Drago didn't know if Bruno had found out the original builder or owner of the palazzo but doubted it would have had such rarefied antecedents.

An inveterate smoker even in such unfashionable times, Inspector Drago's immediate thought on scrutinising the bleak wintery landscape of the palazzo car park was to reach for a cigarette.

His second non politically correct gesture was to offer them to his colleagues.

To his surprise, all acquiesced.

'Didn't Inspector Bruno already search this area with the GPR?' Drago asked the constables dressed in their winter coats as the little group exited the warmth of the Land Rover and stood smoking at the car park entrance.

'Yes, sir,' they replied. 'We looked everywhere.'

'Well, I am doing some old-fashioned ground penetrating radar now,' Drago muttered defiantly to himself as much as the assembled police officers turned labourers.

Sending his colleagues off to see what they could find, he wandered around the car park deep in thought, head down, concluded his constables who kept looking back at him to see if he was faring any better.

Dom Drago looked at shuttered up windows, looked into the sky, along the ground, at ornate cellar doors that must have led somewhere.

Above him, seabirds circled in wide circles, cawing and

crying in the bitter air.

Being an educated man, Domenico Drago knew "Seagulls" were in fact Terns, Guillemots and Petrels amongst other long winged avian wanderers of the oceans.

He still couldn't help but wonder, were they were laughing at him?

Bastard birds, he concluded, an anger now growing from nowhere to fill the inspector's soul.

He'd bloody show them, almost raising his fist at them but thought better of it though the high-flying birds continued to jeer at him.

The inspector walked back towards his colleagues as they started to shiver waiting for him by their police car holding shovels blade down to the pavement.

He then stopped in his tracks and focused slowly, lighting up another cigarette again for inspiration.

He was still getting barracked from the hecklers over his head.

With growing frustration he looked to his left, away from his officers at the boarded-up car park attendant's booth, a length of coiled rope left to the elements next to it.

The similar ropes on the heraldic crest he had spied earlier had given him an idea.

'Did anyone search there?' he asked the officers indicating the care-taker's booth.

'Don't think so sir,' they replied. 'The old guy was in it at the time I think,' one explained as they slowly approached it.

'Let's open it officer,' Drago said as they stood in front of the boarded-up door.

Officer Carboni retrieved a crowbar from the car boot and forced open the booth door.

All four then looked into a tatty dark interior with one old seat and an electric fire nestled on a low wooden shelf.

'Get this lot out including the carpet,' Drago commanded them.

A little pile of furniture, junk mostly, rose next to the empty booth as the officers tossed out items getting in the way of their search.

Drago then looked in, armed with a spade and shoved its blade into the thin crumbly concrete floor and immediately struck something metallic.

A little bit of digging ensued as rubble was deposited next to the junk already removed.

'Look, an old man-hole cover,' Drago said breathlessly. 'Carboni, come with me in the car back to headquarters and call someone over here who can open man-holes and bring torches okay?

'I'll make the call sir,' he replied.

'Prestimone you stay here with Lucio and guard the booth.'

'Sir,' the constables acknowledged, one on his way out, grateful to be getting out of the cold; the other two stealing themselves for a cold half hour on guard duty even in great coats and fur hats.

*

Returning to the police station, Inspector Drago found a rather thin file on his desk along with a short welcome note from DS Chilabon.

Dom Drago called her in as soon as he had settled in his chair and caught up on his emails.

Introductions were polite and business-like.

Neither had worked with the other previously.

Jordi Bruno was the only inspector Amanda had dealt with – now here was an unknown quantity but the job had to be done.

As if by magic, Amanda's mobile buzzed.

It was Deputy Director Nerone.

He got straight to the point as Dom Drago stood by listening.

'I called Inspector Drago to take over the investigation for the present DS Chilabon,' he said like he was reading the news. Chilabon hoped Nerone appreciated how awkward things were. She was ready to cooperate of course but she was a detective sergeant.

'Not because I doubt your capabilities DS Chilabon,' Nerone was explaining from his office in L'Aquila, the regional capital. 'But I want an inspector level policeman pursuing Ella's murderer and I was recommended Inspector Drago.'

'Yes, sir,' Chilabon replied. 'I will work as hard with the inspector as I would have with Inspector Bruno,' she added.

'I know you will,' Nerone switched to a more smooth tone, complimenting the detective sergeant on successful previous investigations. 'Inspector Bruno has suggested several leads I gather to yourself?'

'Inspector Bruno asked me to find out more about the Palazzo Gran Sasso,' Chilabon replied to Deputy Nerone while picking up a file and opening it in front of Inspector Drago on his desk.

'Very good, see where the search goes then,' Nerone replied before wishing them both well and ending the call.

'Right then DS Chilabon what have we got here? A thin file for such a big building,' Drago commented though not as a criticism of her work rate as he was at pains to point out.

'I think I found something at the Palazzo Gran Sasso earlier this morning so we shall see what comes to light after the car park manhole cover has been lifted.'

'Some these files were passed from Ella Frantoni via Inspector Bruno,' Amanda explained which caused them both to momentarily pause and consider Ella's violent end. 'I found some duplicate files in Pescara Municipal archives of what Ella had also found sir. There are seventeen apartments in Palazzo Gran Sasso listed as occupied, all as tenants,' she continued. 'But, I couldn't find any copies of tenancy agreements or even a complete list of tenants, but all, bar the English teacher Celestini put in the apartment overlooking the Corso have apparently been there decades.' Then, 'this was weird, sir. There was no record of Contessa Di Lanciano occupying any apartment. I cross-referenced it with a fifth-floor plan from the 50's Ella got from the archives. Guess what?'

'Don't tell me,' Drago responded waiting for the DS's next trick.

'Yes, sir, her apartment doesn't exist.

The plan shows one big apartment on that floor.

'It's been subdivided at some point.'

'One way of putting it,' Drago replied as he sat back digesting the news. 'Not especially illegal on first viewing although suspicious. Signor Celestini may have the paperwork documenting this,' he added cagily. 'But, I can't see him volunteering any of it DS Chilabon?' Drago asked somewhat awkwardly, 'Can you find out how much Celestini *pere* paid for the palazzo and when he bought it? And, it is possible to put a current valuation on it?'

'Why do you want that sir?' Chilabon asked.

'To get an idea of the size of Signor Celestini's assets,' Drago replied.

139

'Yes, sir,' Chilabon turned and started to exit the room. 'Where are you doing now inspector?' she asked, standing by the door as he got up to put on his jacket.

'I am going back to the palazzo to see progress on lifting the manhole cover. And see if Ella Frantoni's iPhone can still show any documents she photographed?' Drago called over to Amanda's desk as he walked through the Criminal Investigation Unit area.

Amanda, on the phone, gave him a thumbs up.

*

Nine forty five p.m.

And so, a couple of hours later two council workmen with a block and tackle from an accompanying crane on a flatbed truck were gingerly lifting the heavy rusty manhole cover, not having been moved for many years clearly.

Inspector Drago, drinking his third espresso, watched anxiously from a cafe opposite moving over to the site as soon as workman gave him the thumbs up. Manhole cover duly deposited on the ground, Dom Drago and Officer Prestimone shone their torches into the depths of the hole – a rusty ladder visible on one side.

Both police torches then aligned on a collection of dirty large objects ten feet or so down crumpled on rubble and debris accumulated from earlier building work. A pair of feet seemed to be sticking out from the debris.

Bruno sighed audibly, realising that their quest might be over.

'Okay, get the fire-brigade here Carboni,' he shouted over to the policeman watching from the police car. 'Soon as possible tell them, and let's see what we've got. I'll call forensics.'

Soon after, a fire engine and ambulance temporarily blocked the whole of the narrow road in front of Palazzo Gran Sasso while several fireman, after letting the forensics technician photograph the remains *in situ,* gingerly winched up what had been found from its resting place at the bottom of the drain. A black body bag then transported the remains in the ambulance to the forensics laboratory where Inspector Drago and pathologist Ener were then waiting. The former smoking outside in the car park while the latter wearing a white forensic suit and mask and carrying a clipboard directed technicians to remove the body for an investigation and autopsy.

*

Later that day, Inspector Drago telephoned Jordi Bruno at home informing him of the second body retrieved from the car park, or more accurately the drain, of the Palazzo Gran Sasso. In Drago's eyes, the grim discovery vindicated his friend as a nosey copper whose hunch that the palazzo hid additional secrets had been proved correct.

There was still the job of formally identifying the body. How that person was murdered. And, when they were deposited in the sad lonely place?

The second soldier accompanying Major Molina back in 1944 was a likely candidate, according to police sources.

Jordi Bruno, listening quietly, then wanted to know any update on his girlfriend's murder.

'Murderer's vehicle, a black Volvo, was found abandoned at the bottom of a steep brook,' Drago informed him. 'A passer-by contacted the station to say he saw a tall man in dark clothes walking away quickly though probably the car was pushed over the ledge rather than being driven over. No plates or CCTV. We're still looking. Might be able to retrieve photos from Ella's phone,' Drago said finishing up.

'Talk to Celestini,' Bruno said after a pause. 'He's key to all this.'

'Don't worry inspector. You rest up and leave it to me.'

*

'You can see why the victim had no chance of surviving the impact inspector,' the foreman of the police car pound pointed out the crumpled driver's seat in the battered Skoda Felicia.

Dom Drago looked over the chaotic site of Ella's death – a lump in his throat would not go away.

DS Chilabon came over to look.

The awful sight of the seatbelt hanging by the door with no sign of having been used told its own story.

'I can't believe someone like Signora Frantoni wouldn't wear a seatbelt, in this day and age,' Drago said finally, stepping back to view the crumpled roof and then the smashed in front end of Ella's car.

'All I can say inspector,' Guiseppi Nero interjected, dressed in his dirty brown overalls and flat cap getting out a clipboard out to wave under Drago's eyes, 'is that she temporarily took it off.'

'Why would she do that?' the inspector asked.

'Her phone was found on the floor of the car,' Nero pointed out in the report. 'If you look carefully inspector,' he added leading the two police officers round to the other side of the car. 'You can see the plastic cradle is cracked but not as a result of the crash as far as we can see. I don't see a car crash knocking the phone out ordinarily.'

Drago and Chilabon peered at the broken phone cradle.

Drago sighed again followed by his assistant as the circumstances Nero demonstrated that resulted in Ella losing her life were laid bare.

'If she had maybe left her phone on the floor and retrieved it when she got home she might have survived inspector,' Guiseppi finished up.

'Someone did smash into the back of her car deliberately so!' Drago reminded the technician.

'I agree if she hadn't been distracted by her dropped phone.'

'Will you put that in your report signor?' Drago asked.

'Shouldn't I inspector?' Nero asked with genuine concern.

*

Ronnie's midweek evening lesson at the Comune was unlike any lesson he had previously taught there.

A sombre mood prevailed, not least because of the murder of Ella Frantoni who was known to some of Cabot's students, themselves also employed at the Commune.

The discovery of the second body under the car park attendant's booth at the Palazzo Gran Sasso was also covered on the evening news.

Ronnie thought about Anna's uncle, sitting on top of that poor soul's lonely tomb all those years without knowing? He shuddered slightly wondering what Anna would also make of it as he hadn't spoken to her for a while.

Life went on and so did English lessons Cabot decided, even though no one was in the mood for them. His attempt to try and continue the English conversation lesson wasn't helped by the fact that Signor Orazio Mancetti normally the life and soul of the lesson was particularly taciturn and excused himself from retiring to the bar at the end of the lesson.

It was probably just as well Ronnie didn't know that it was his student and friend Orazio who had been monitoring Frantoni's phone calls and indeed given had Darius, Ronnie's employer, the make and number plate of her car.

Cabot would have got seriously angry.

*

Later on in the evening, Ronnie found himself with Mauro propped up at the bar along with another student of his, Giani Tedesco who ran a Jewellery business in Chieti town centre.

Conversation was inevitable about Darius, who Cabot had to admit, he hadn't seen for days. The implications of the second body of the suspected soldier found under the care-taker's booth at the Palazzo Gran Sasso were also pondered. Beyond a name in an old book, it had been hard to formally identify the corpse as there seemed to have no living descendants according to police investigations.

Giani, who was particularly well-informed of what happened locally commented to Cabot in almost a whisper that Mauro concurred with, that Italians were still not that far from events of 1945 compared to people like the British, who had undoubtedly also suffered in the war but had one advantage over Italians in that they had never been an occupied country.

Giani's father indeed, had moved to Abruzzo after the war for a better life for him and his family than the impoverished Sicily where the family originated from.

His father had taken over a building where the previous

owners had fled for whatever reason and the Italian government, being anxious to restore some semblance of economic life to Chieti, granted them ownership by default. The previous owners were rumoured to have been Jewish, Giani said but as no-one came forward after the war to claim the building, it became in time Giani's family property.

All Ronnie could do was drink his free lagers and listen quietly, previously unaware that the society around him had been as pragmatic post war as circumstances dictated. As long as Abruzzese sleeping dogs were left lying and people got on with their lives building a new economy, then so be it, he concluded.

Had Ella Frantoni and indeed the lost soldiers from 1944 lost their lives because they had threatened to upturn one of these 'dogs?' The three patrons at the bar thought sadly, silently, on this thought as they nursed their lagers.

*

Inspector Drago had rescinded for the time being, his order to find and bring in for questioning Signor Darius Celestini. He wanted to gather more information and see where the investigation went. Darius wasn't going anywhere after all.

Drago's police radio crackled into life as he stepped out of the police station to walk home to his hotel room. It was Station Sergeant Degrelli.

'We've found the taxi driver the murder suspect used after dumping the Volvo,' he said. 'It's an address out at Mantini, a small suburb on the main highway to the Adriatic coast.

'Okay thanks,' Drago responded. 'Get the taxi company owner to meet me at the taxi office first thing tomorrow morning with the driver. Let's see what he has to say.'

'The iPhone sir from Signorina Frantoni,' Degrelli continued, 'is useless. Forensics can't retrieve any photos from its memory.'

Drago cursed quietly.

Friday 24 February – Eight Thirty a.m.

That morning, in bitter foul weather with a white hoar-frost covering the roofs and vegetation of the whole area, a bright red Alfa Romeo police car with Inspector Drago and Detective Sergeant Chilabon turned into a frozen muddy taxi company car park in the fairly shabby industrial area of Martini.

DS Chilabon, demonstrating manual dexterity dating back to her younger gymnastic days, picked out the quickest path through the frozen oil, mud and other unsavouries lurking on the ground to the large rubber mat outside the taxi office door.

Inspector Drago however, resorted to a more straight forward clomping approach, hoping his expensive black leather shoes would not along with the rest of him disappear into an unsuspecting pothole.

After hasty introductions at the now open office door – with the manager and the young driver Drago wished to question – a student by all reckoning, Iani Stanieri – all four went inside and out of the cold.

Soon, the police and the driver were ensconced in the manager's office behind the taxi communication desk; a thick wooden table sporting two laptops and innumerable mobile phones, manned by a large unshaven man in a white T-shirt and braces who didn't seem to realise that the wonders of modern technology meant you could talk into a microphone instead of shouting into it. Stanieri's manager, a scruffily dressed man about ten years older than the student, sat next to the big taxi driver

147

coordinator, his elbows on the table and smoking with a detached air, seemingly indifferent to having been temporarily evicted from his office.

Drago reached into his greatcoat pocket and produced a passport sized black and white photo of the suspect. 'Recognise him?' he asked the taxi driver.

'It was *dark*, inspector,' Stanieri replied shifting awkwardly in his chair and pulling a face. 'His cap was pulled down and he banged on my car bonnet as I was pulling into the rank here. Wouldn't take no for an answer but gave me a nice tip though.'

'Which seat did he sit in?'

'Front seat passenger,' the driver replied.

'Well then, you must have got sight of his face?'

'His age?'

'Weight?'

'Come on, son,' Inspector Drago moaned irritably, moved up a gear and reckoning he could make something of telling the university authorities a student of theirs was moonlighting. 'What could the university do with Signor Stanieri DS Chilabon, if they found out one of their students was driving on the quiet and probably uninsured ?' Drago asked, turning to his companion in her winter coat but then returning a steely glare at the shifty witness.

'Kicked off the course, repay fees to university, legal action, plenty they can do, plus…,' she replied in a deadpan voice.

'Hey, hey, wait a minute!' Iani interrupted, 'Look, he was wearing a fur winter coat and gloves. I didn't look at him close up, give me a break please!'

'What colour coat?'

'Black,' the driver quickly replied.

'Is this the guy you picked up then Signor Stanieri? Look

carefully now and take your time,' Drago told him while looking over Stanieri's shoulder in exasperation towards the continual shouted dialogues in the taxi communications room.

'Maybe it's him,' Iani said slowly as he scrutinised the photo. 'The silhouette, I remember his silhouette,' Stanieri said finally putting the photo down on the desk.

'How could you see his silhouette if it was dark?'

'Oncoming car headlights lit it up a bit I remember,' Stanieri offered up.

'Swear in court?' Drago asked.

'I don't know, maybe,' Stanieri said quietly.

The policeman sighed with exasperation. 'You're not being helpful sir,' he said with an air of slight menace. 'Where did you drop this guy then?'

'At the Post Office on the sea-front in "Franca". He paid cash and gave me a nice tip too,' Stanieri smiled, for the first time.

'How did he pay?' Drago asked.

'Cash,' came the reply. 'In fact…' and Stanieri fumbled in his wallet, 'because it was after I had cashed up, I didn't put it in my takings. The twenty-euro note is here,' he said making to pull it out.

'What good is that to me if he was wearing gloves?' Drago asked arms flung wide, almost clipping his colleague on her ear.

'He took his glove *off* inspector to get his bank note out,' Stanieri said slowly as if he was talking to a child.

'Wait!' Drago jumped up and grabbed the wallet. 'We may have a finger print here then.' Drago carefully took the rest of the cash and bank cards out and handed them to the taxi driver. 'Thank you for your information sir. Now, we're getting somewhere. We'll keep this for now,' he continued, handing the wallet to DS Chilabon who produced a clear plastic bag to

149

transport the said article to a forensic lab. 'I also want your car keys. We are impounding your taxi to check it forensically too,' Drago added.

'The taxi is my income,' Stanieri protested lamely but Drago wasn't listening.

'My colleagues will contact you today. Don't worry Signor Stanieri, you'll get everything back as soon as we've concluded our investigations. Let's get out of here now Detective Sergeant,' Drago said already out of his seat and heading for the door without proffering any thanks to their interviewee.

Chilabon nodded curtly as she exited behind her boss leaving the hapless taxi driver standing with arms down by his sides and downcast expression on his face – not even offered a cigarette by the inspector as he lit up as soon as he was outside.

Chilabon's iPhone pinged a message from her contact at the land registry in Chieti. They told her that Celestini's father had paid the equivalent of about a hundred thousand dollars for the palazzo in the 60's as it was then very run down but didn't have an original bill of purchase; only a note in a general file for property purchases for the relevant year.

Today the palazzo was worth several million euros, the note went on to say.

'Hmm,' mused Drago again as he heard the news. 'Wonder where Celestini senior got the money for that?'

*

<u>One p.m.</u>
Anna had asked to meet Ronnie at a little cafe just outside Pescara university main gate at lunchtime, an hour or so before his afternoon lessons.

150

He couldn't stay more than twenty minutes or so before hopping on a bus over the road to Chieti Scalo.

She was sitting at a table next to the window, waving when she saw him enter the cafe's front door.

Soon after, amid the din of a busy student restaurant area, Ronnie was sat down opposite her, realising, but not commenting on the fact that she had put some make-up on.

In the middle of the day, between lectures.

Mmm, he thought.

She wasn't smiling though but Cabot continued to be drawn to her lilac-coloured lipstick and soft pale features peeping out of her embroidered woollen hat.

'My uncle's mental health isn't good at the moment,' she said sighing, putting her coffee cup down forcing Ronnie to focus away from her lips to her anxieties. 'Everyone in my family is worried but he won't talk about it.'

'He must have been happy the second body was found?' Ronnie asked. 'Probably the missing soldier that had disappeared with his sister in the Jeep? Didn't you see it on TV?'

'I saw it,' Anna replied, 'but I don't know how much notice my uncle took of it. He's just kind of switched off.'

'You should have told Inspector Bruno about what your uncle found in my old bedroom ceiling straight away,' Cabot told her quietly, sipping his cappuccino brought over to him from the service counter.

'I know,' she responded awkwardly. 'I don't know if he found anything else apart from dog tags – none of us do because he won't tell us,' she said.

'Well, that poor woman Ella Frantoni from the Comune who was murdered,' Ronnie continued. 'there might be a connection, the TV report said. You mustn't talk about your uncle's situation casually with anyone at university Anna,' he said, holding her arms with his hands and looking into her frowning face.

She then forced a wan smile at him but sighed as she slumped slightly in her seat.

That meant she probably already had, sighed Cabot silently as he caught her body language's subliminal message of inevitable defeat.

He wouldn't let that happen again, he told himself.

*

Dom Drago along with Amanda Chilabon decided Jordi Bruno needed checking up on so after picking up a pizza take-away from a local pizza restaurant soon arrived at Bruno's small apartment in Francavilla Al Mare.

'It's the best eatery for miles around in my opinion, sir,' DS Chilabon said as she brought one of the two hot pizza boxes close to her nose. 'I think Jordi will know it well,' she added as Drago parked before turning off the police Land Rover engine and took his seat belt off.

*

Inspector Jordi Bruno was dressed in a grey tracksuit, not unlike the prison uniform some of the old lags wore he had put away down the years would have been wearing at the same time not a million miles away.

Indicative of a man who hadn't been outside recently Chilabon surmised rather than a fashion statement.

Drago and Chilabon greeted their colleague warmly with the pizzas and a bottle of local Monte Pulciano.

Bruno attempted a smile along with a muted greeting before leading them through the living room to his balcony overlooking the crashing tides of the Adriatic not a hundred yards away.

'It was good of you to come,' Bruno said as he picked two more wine glasses out of a kitchen cabinet.

'We wanted to check you were all right mate,' Domenico offered as he placed the pizza boxes on the balcony table. 'I wasn't going to call you to book an appointment neither!' he added smiling and asking the host for a bottle opener.

'Protocol means I am not discussing the case with you in detail Jordi but I just wanted to make sure you knew myself and Amanda along with all the unit are working tirelessly to bring Ella's killer to justice,' Dom Drago said as all three were sat down half watching the sea, half wondering *how* the case would eventually be resolved.

'I blame myself as you can imagine,' Jordi said quietly as he slowly took half a pizza slice in a rolled piece of grease proof paper.

The other two sat anxiously wondering how far this thought was controlling their friend.

'You mustn't sir,' Amanda replied with a glass of wine in one hand. 'She knew it was a risk to help the investigation. She was murdered because she wanted to do the right thing sir.'

Bruno sighed, putting down his glass on the table. 'That doesn't help me,' he added. 'I felt terrible talking to her parents. There is a terrible emptiness…'

Bruno put his forehead in one hand while Drago put an arm round his shoulder.

'We are all thinking of you sir,' Chilabon said quietly from the other side of the table.

'I am not looking forward to the funeral Mandy,' Jordi said looking up, red-eyed. 'Whenever that is.'

Saturday 26 February – 8.24 a.m.

Inspector Domenico Drago sent two Carabinieri round to Darius Celestini's English language school early that morning, where he duly was apprehended and then escorted back to Drago's office for a formal interview. He already had the dog tag photographs from Anna she had sent by email attachment. Drago was in uncharted waters now however, with Chieti's great and the good but his persistence was there for all personnel to see.

Darius Celestini had requested and been granted a lawyer to sit in the interview with him.

It didn't go unnoticed to those who knew him at the police station that Signor Celestini was unusually badly dressed in what looked like a tracksuit.

Celestini finally sat down in the interview room in the basement accompanied by his lawyer, Signor Innocente Lollis. A small round man with owl-like glasses balanced on a pudgy nose – the suitability or even the irony of his first name for his clients was not lost on Drago who sat down opposite them at Inspector Bruno's office table.

He called Chilabon to come and sit in with him and observe the interview.

Darius Celestini hadn't known that Ella Frantoni's iPad had been destroyed as well as anything incriminating.

She had perished for nothing in the fiery car crash the previous Tuesday.

154

*

'Signor Celestini,' Drago started when all four were sat down. 'I am sitting in for my colleague Inspector Giordano Bruno. He has been,' a pause for Darius to appreciate Drago's sentiments, 'badly affected by the murder of his close friend while she was driving home.'

'What's that go to do with me?' Darius replied shrugging his shoulders indignantly like a spoilt teenager. Then, 'Why did you have to dig up my car park attendant's booth?' Ignoring the fact that a body had been retrieved, he continued. 'I hope you are going to put it all back when you're finished and...'

'What's it got to do with *you?*' Drago interrupted, flinging back the question with the mock cry of the afflicted as he looked up at the ceiling. 'This is to do with you or you wouldn't have broken into a student's room and taken items retrieved from a concealed space in one of your properties' ceiling!'

Those dog tags,' Drago said slamming the table with his hand clutching the photocopied picture of them, causing the other three to blink. 'You were recognised on the student accommodation block stairs by the student whose room you broke into, so I can do you for burglary and obstructing an investigation signor,' Drago finished up seeing if the interviewee opposite was registering what he said.

'Ah,' Darius said slowly. 'Thought I recognised the little madam. A family of thieves! Those tags belong to me,' Darius replied defiantly. A pause. 'I was taking them back,' his tone changing to a more languid one.

'How did you know Tomaso Scilaci found dog tags signor?'

'I didn't actually,' Darius replied slowly, 'but from all the carry-on I knew he had found *something* so I wanted to see for myself and found out her student address. The tags are now at my villa.'

A pause.

'I have a lot of friends hereabouts inspector,' Celestini said carefully looking to intimidate Drago.

'My officers will go over there now and retrieve them as they are evidence,' Drago told Celestini before continuing. 'I don't care how many friends you have signor. If they break the law I'll be feeling their collars too. It is my supposition that you have access to confidential information from the Comune Liberal Party branch, of which I am told, you are a member. I will find out who your contact is, make no mistake and make it my business to lock them up for perverting the course of justice and anything else I can think of!' Inspector Drago responded leaning forward attempting to unnerve the man opposite. 'Are you a Freemason signor?'

Celestini snorted.

'I'll take that as a yes,' the policeman replied mentally ticking the box and hopefully heaping more pressure on the suspect.

'Four nights ago,' Drago continued, 'a car was forced off the road to Bucchianico killing the driver. Vehicle registration records we have consulted in Rome say that one of your cars is a black Volvo, like the car that caused the death of the poor girl driving. Where were you that night around 6.30–7 p.m.?'

'I was…'

'We know you weren't at home in Termoli so don't bother lying,' Drago interrupted, 'because Inspector Bruno sent two uniforms round there. School was also closed.'

'I was driving along the coast towards Vasto. I wanted to think.'

'Really?' Drago sat back, arms folded. 'Which car were you driving that cold dark night?'

'My Mercedes,' he replied.

'Where was it parked during the day?'

'In a side street near the school,' Darius replied. 'Via Gennaro Ravizza.'

'What happened to the Volvo you owned?'

'I sold it?'

'To whom?'

'Can't remember. It was a cash sale,' Darius responded.

'Give me a name? A receipt? I want proof!' Drago shouted.

'Inspector,' the round lawyer Lollis suddenly roused himself. 'My client is here to help you not hinder you. You have cast aspersions on his character so please present evidence. Otherwise there is no need for him to be here and insulted.'

'Aspersions? Speculations?' Drago replied throwing the lawyer's words back at him. 'Your client is here to help police matters and, how can I phrase it, *cast light in dark places*. At the moment I am getting a load of nonsense from your client.'

Darius sat opposite, unmoved by Drago's deliberate irony on dark places.

Inspector Drago then turned the page in the file on the desk in front of him and showed him a black and white passport type photo of a man in military uniform.

'Who's this?' Drago asked Darius.

Celestini said nothing, but immediately sat up straight, pursing his lips – the lawyer craning his fat neck over to get a view of the exhibit, biting his lip as an obvious sign he was working out a favourable explanation on behalf of his client.

'I'll tell you then,' Drago said. 'It's your father isn't it? He said quietly with a forced smile.

'And?' Darius shrugged almost painfully, letting out a long breath.

'This picture came out of the government archives in Pescara. Our government is still pursuing war crimes suspects, even today!' Drago said, looking for a reaction in the man opposite.

No reaction from the aforesaid.

The inspector continued, 'Your father fought with the MVSN militia on the German side did he not?'

'Why do you need to harass my client like this?' Lollis asked across his client who seemed to have shrunk ever so slightly into his chair. 'These events happened many years ago before my client was even born!' Lollis continued, looking at Darius sitting stock still next to him.

'I am not harassing him,' Drago replied with restraint. 'I want some truth even after such a long time. Anti-fascist Margaretta, her fellow fighter, the late Contessa. I demand truth on their behalf too!'

A pause while all assembled noisily collected their thoughts.

'I think his father,' Inspector Drago continued, looking at the lawyer but pointing at Celestini, 'is responsible for the two bodies we have found in the Palazzo Gran Sasso. We know that the captured officer, the one in the photograph here, was being taken by the allies to Sulmona for interrogation after being captured near Francavilla in 1944. We have it from documentation that this same officer wasn't properly searched as circumstantial evidence points to him having probably a concealed Luger pistol with which the officer later overpowered the two soldiers guarding him, one of whom was your former maintenance man's aunt.

'Wish I had never have employed the fat bastard,' Darius

muttered under his breath.

'What?' Drago leaned over closer.

Darius shrugged.

'Having gained control of the jeep, I suspect the Major drove it or forced one of the soldiers to drive to Chieti instead of Sulmona right? Why the Palazzo Gran Sasso?

'Because the officer owned it or at least was familiar with the building apparently.'

'Why?'

'He had been the same officer I suspect who had shot at Chieti residents from the same top floor apartment your English employee Ronnie Cabot was living in.'

Darius still sitting still like a sullen school child in the head master's office, said nothing as another profound silence descended upon Drago's office as cobwebby memories were suddenly pushed into the frantic light of day.

Four pairs of eyes focused on the small passport shaped photograph of the officer lying in the middle of the desk, wearing a black military officer's hat with a trace of a smile playing on his mouth.

Inspector Drago had finished for now.

'DS Chilabon, escort Signor Celestini out of the building please?' Drago asked, getting up to leave.

'Yes sir,' she replied as all four noisily and wordlessly pushed chairs away and made their exits.

'You'll be hearing from us very soon signor. By the way,' Drago continued, talking to their backsides but managing to stop lawyer and person of interest in their tracks. 'Why was the Contessa's sub-divided apartment not marked on the fifth-floor plan of the palazzo Signor Celestini?'

Darius Celestini couldn't help but smile. 'No idea,' he

retorted, half turning round. 'I didn't know that. Not illegal though. She still paid all her taxes.'

Drago knew Celestini was lying, and badly.

*

<u>1.25 p.m.</u>

It was Bernie on the line as Ronnie was walking towards the language centre in Chieti Scalo when his mobile went off.

'Hi Ronnie, have you heard about Signor Darius?'

Cabot hadn't so Bernie, who was closer to the centre of the action than him, related how Darius, dressed more for a workout than the office, had been taken away that morning by two policemen from his office at the main school building. No one had ever seen anything like it amongst the long serving Italian English teachers as an outsider like Bernie was soon informed.

Ronnie wasn't sure if he was surprised or not.

In Ronnie's opinion Darius' troubles and indeed Ronnie's troubles had started when *his* boiler had packed up – if Darius had properly maintained his property then…? Then what? The body may have been discovered ten years later? Or Never?

'See you round Bernie and thanks for letting me know,' Ronnie replied finally, opening the school office door ready to greet Tiziana who probably already knew anyway.

*

'My colleague Inspector Bruno tells me you think a ghost murdered the Contessa?' Drago said in a flat voice down the phone to Ronnie Cabot, catching him during a break in evening English lessons to a group of adult earners, most of whom were

160

there to *actually* work and not network.

'I am not judging you Signor Cabot by the way,' the inspector continued before Ronnie could comment. 'If that's what you saw then that's fine with me. All I ask is that you may provide me with a witness statement if you would be so kind?'

'It's crazy inspector I know but I don't have another explanation,' Cabot replied still feeling defensive about what he had encountered. He was sitting in the language school office chair opposite secretary Tiziana while his secrets were being spilled out for all the world to know. 'Your police artist drew a *back* view of the figure that old woman who cleaned there saw. I never *saw* the back of the figure but it looked very similar to the *front* of the one I saw.' Then speculating a little, Cabot continued. 'Do you reckon anyone can be *frightened* to death, inspector?'

'I work in the concrete world Signor Cabot so I have no idea to be sure,' Drago replied. 'But, it is interesting that this figure was only seen once the body behind your boiler was discovered.'

'The old bat said I had released her,' Cabot said in irritated tone causing Tiziana to sit up and listen at her desk.

'Bat?' Dom Drago laughed down the phone at Ronnie's slang as he corrected himself,

'Sorry, inspector, old lady, I mean,' Cabot corrected himself to a more serious demeanour.

'Well, Signor Cabot,' Drago continued. 'I may get some raised eyebrows for believing you but I do. The Contessa also had some kind of relationship with the Celestini family but I haven't discovered exactly what it was yet. You will see this story in the press in a few days probably,' Drago continued, oozing familiarity as Ronnie was one of his official witnesses.

Tiziana moved a bit closer to Ronnie hoping to hear what more of what he was being told.

161

'The old cleaner also said *it* was waiting for justice,' Cabot told the policeman. 'Perhaps that was what happened in that poor soul's world when she visited the Contessa's apartment. How could the Contessa give her justice?' he asked finishing up.

The inspector had no answer again so goodbyes were exchanged before Drago hung up.

He wanted to keep up momentum on the case, so called Station Sergeant Degrelli at the police station front desk on his way back to the hotel.

'Were there were any CCTV cameras on via Gennaro Ravizza we can check to see if Signor Celestini's parked Mercedes could be identified as parked there the day of Ella's murder?'

He also asked Degrelli to get onto the forensic lab first thing in the morning to see if any fingerprints could be salvaged from the banknote the taxi driver had offered.

Thirdly he wanted a DNA sample retrieved from the Contessa's body but wouldn't say why.

Degrelli listened attentively, notebook in hand – quietly unassuming but with an air of authority, not to be crossed lightly.

Just the kind of policeman both Inspector Drago and Bruno before him had concluded, that was vital as a bridge between the ordinary citizenry (of which both inspectors counted themselves a part) and state power.

Could Drago get Degrelli to work in his Rome office instead?

No, Bruno his colleague would complain to the President of the Republic himself if Drago pinched his best station sergeant!

*

162

Since losing his main occupation monitoring the car-park at Palazzo Gran Sasso, Tomaso Scilaci spent most of his days at home watching TV and in the local cafe down the street playing backgammon with fellow retired souls.

He had a pension so wasn't broke but to be taken away from the scene of the discovery of his aunt's body and away from the inquest rankled him. He did, however, have a couple of treasures saved from his frantic burglary in Ronnie Cabot's old apartment which periodically he got out and savoured when everyone else in the household was asleep. His fingers lingered over the metallic object with its short barrel as he lost himself in his tearful thoughts of his poor aunt's last terrifying moments in the chaos of war. Then he became angry towards his late employer pushing his bottom lip around with his right index finger.

The casualness of the way he, Signor Tomaso Scilaci had been tossed aside when perceived by this man of being taking what was rightfully his?'

What a nerve! His family had fought for this country!

He had better watch out, Tomaso thought or he, Tomaso would come looking for revenge for himself and his aunt.

*

'Signor Celestini, it seems to me highly unlikely that you didn't know what your father's involvement was with the Palazzo Gran Sasso though much of what I and my fellow investigator, Inspector Bruno have found out, dates to the end of the last war before you were born. However,' and here Drago leaned forward to look directly at Darius, 'you have not been honest with the local police as I have shown and have obstructed the police when it suited you.'

163

'I have been as helpful as I can,' Darius replied coldly.

Lollis, his lawyer was sitting next to his client in the same police station interview room where they had recently clashed, jumped (metaphorically at least), to his defence.

This Celestini sitting awkwardly in front of the inspector wasn't the busy affable local businessman Celestini, always on the phone doing deals.

This Celestini needed to get these people to leave him alone and let him get on with his life.

He hadn't buried anyone in the palazzo but what could he have done differently?

Denied his father?

Turned him in?

No one was taking the Palazzo Gran Sasso off him, that was for certain.

'I and indeed, my colleagues have wondered why a Contessa would be living in a poky apartment in your palazzo,' Inspector Drago wondered out loud. 'She offered no clues to my colleagues then, after her death, Inspector Bruno's officers found this in one of her drawers,' Drago said looking directly at Darius and showing him the old photo of a much younger Contessa and the Major in an embrace during some wartime party, fascist insignia clearly visible on his officer's hat and shoulder epaulettes.

'Italians had to choose sides as you well know,' Darius said, ignoring Drago's pointed question about the status of the Contessa. 'My father chose Il Duce's view of the world. Whose side did *your* family choose? Huh? 'What's your story Inspector?' Celestini asked looking up suddenly annoyed, into the Inspector's eyes. 'Grandfather helping the Americans 'liberate' as you would say? Or skulking in the hills shagging sheep every night?'

The policeman snorted with derision, choosing not to belt the man opposite helping him with his enquiry. 'My family didn't pick up a palazzo or have any bodies hidden on their property!' Drago shot back with a subdued laugh.

'Well, don't assume my father shares a similar world view to me. This is the 21st century not 1944,' Celestini responded with a weary air. He had been at police headquarters, 'waiting' for the inspector's interview for over an hour and was now extremely irritated at doing Lollis' job for him. He had paid him well enough.

'I am not accusing you of anything connected to this photograph,' Drago replied, noting that Celestini had used the present tense *"shares"* instead of the past tense the policeman had expected to hear.

Had Celestini slipped up?

'I am merely interested in your comments,' Drago continued regaining his composure and focusing on the picture in the middle of the table.

'I didn't know such a photo existed,' Darius Celestini replied truthfully for once. I have no photos in my possession showing my father in uniform. You want to know where my father is? Come and visit him at my farm in the hills above Alterna-Pescara river.'

This offer from Darius caused an immediate raising of eyebrows from Inspector Drago before a quick response.

'Fine. We will go with you tomorrow morning as soon as I can organise a couple of cars,' Drago replied emphatically, getting to his feet. 'Meanwhile, Signor Celestini, you are free to go,' he finished looking at the round lawyer as he stood up to protest.

'You will have to charge him then or leave him alone,'

lawyer Lollis said as he turned and smiled at Darius who seemed strangely calm upon hearing the inspector's pronouncement. Drago decided not to share the fact that he had requested a DNA sample from the Contessa's remains.

He would hold that in reserve for now.

*

'Death was by multiple injuries resulting from the car crash,' Pathologist Ener told Bruno and Chilabon as they stood in the Pathologist's office later in the day. Ener showed them an X-ray photograph of the victim's skull area and handed Bruno a report to take away. 'The initial impact of the killer's car would have caused serious whiplash injuries to the victim causing her to lose control of the car. She wasn't wearing her seatbelt either, sadly which may have saved her. Any leads on the murderer inspector?' Ener asked hopefully

'Maybe Patricia. We may have the fingerprint of the suspect but would it be enough to make a charge of murder stick?' Bruno asked his colleague rhetorically. 'We also have a vague description of the suspect from a taxi driver who picked him up but as it all happened in the dark'

'Difficult to see whether the district prosecutor would ever put our suspect in front of a judge Signora Ener, but we're not giving up,' Chilabon added more good news, causing all three to frown.

'Good luck with it then is all I can say,' Pathologist Ener smiled in her white jacket, acknowledging Drago and Chilabon's frowns as they took their leave to return to the police station in Chieti.

'By the way,' Inspector Drago turned and addressed the

166

pathologist as Ener was going back to her office. 'Do you stand by your conclusion that the late Contessa seemed to have been 'frightened to death? Is that your *professional* opinion?'

'Working in scientific investigations, I don't do irrational explanations inspector. But I am at a loss to explain her death, so I fall back on the Sherlock Holmesian conclusion, if I can put it like that!'

'Drago smiled grimly as he exited the building.

*

Lollis picked up the phone and closed his office door.

A youngish man picked up.

'The police are coming up to the farm tomorrow. It shouldn't be a problem should it?'

'No problem,' came the emphatic reply. 'I'll see everything is as it should be.'

Lollis put the phone down with a contented air.

Monday 28 February – 9.05 a.m.

Cesare Frantoni walked into the reception area of the Comune in an angry mood.

The local papers had run riot with speculation as to the motive for his sister's murder which only added to the Frantoni family's anguish. The police investigation was proceeding with a report in the paper that the taxi driver who picked up the murderer had been traced and interviewed but there the leads had for the present, dried up.

The Comune had done nothing to aid the investigation, though there hadn't been anything in particular it had been asked to do. What had Ella's boss, Signor Mancetti done to help?

Nothing, as far as her brother Cesare could see.

But another question burned in Cesare's head.

Had Ella *really* been involved in some sort of espionage with the local police department as the newspapers had speculated? Cesare didn't even know Jordi Bruno had been her boyfriend. Why would he?

'I want to see the party secretary,' Cesare demanded at the Christian Liberal party front desk.

Signora Michele Ceresa, the senior secretary bristled at this intrusion. No one came in here demanding things. She needed to inform Signor Mancetti in his office upstairs.

'*You* will have to wait here,' she stalled coldly, picking up the phone.

A hushed hurried conversation ensued in the broadest dialect

168

with the aim of getting rid of, if not confusing Signor Frantoni. His late sister had been an incomer into Abruzzo and the assumption was that her brother was too and wouldn't understand dialect.

Finally, after more phone conversation in dialect, the phone was put down.

'Signor Mancetti is busy and suggests you make an appointment,' Signora Ceresa suggested blandly.

'I want to see him now!' Cesare was angry now. 'I want to know what he is doing about the death of my sister!'

'You have to leave now,' Ceresa responded in a firm tone with a nod to two security guards sat on wooden chairs by the revolving circular doors that moved round in one direction allowing entry.

'You don't care! You're hiding something!' Cesare shouted up the stairs towards Mancetti's office as he was grabbed by security and propelled towards the doors. The hubbub had attracted the attention of other visitors to the Comune as well as office workers behind Ceresa's desk.

Cesare Frantoni was deposited on his feet in the street just as the snow began to fall.

He was fuming and continued to shout at the now closed main entrance.

It was only a matter of time before the Carabinieri would show up and engage with the angry citizen. Doubtless Signora Ceresa had called them. Gathering himself together, Ella's angry brother slunk away in the snow to plan his next move. He wasn't done with the Christian Liberal Party and its slippery party secretary.

Station Sergeant Degrelli had word from forensics.

First the good news for Inspector Drago.

He had been sent three finger prints retrieved from the bank note, one of which invariably would be the taxi driver's signor Stanieri. The other two? The suspect's? Had to be, thought Degrelli unless the note had been given to the suspect immediately before he had then given it to the taxi driver? Unlikely, mused the station sergeant. Would they have any of these prints on record even?

Then the bad news. There was no working CCTV from the street where Darius Celestini said his Mercedes was parked the day of the murder.

Degrelli printed off the two emails for the inspector to read.

A minute or so later, his attention was then drawn to the picture on Inspector Bruno's desk currently being used by Inspector Drago, as he laid the printed off emails next to it.

There was the head and shoulders black and white photograph of the woman he had seen walk into the very same office!

But it couldn't be.

This woman had disappeared back in 1944.

He looked around furtively while he scrutinised the photo.

He would have to tell the inspector even if he were derided for it.

*

1.04 p.m.

That afternoon, Ronnie Cabot decided to walk past his old home before getting his tram down the hill to Chieti Scalo, just to see if he noticed any changes.

'Well, well,' Cabot exclaimed out loud at no one in

particular.

A new caretaker, a younger version in fact, was standing at the car park barrier in his heavy winter coat and over large hat. This was no Tomaso so no cheery welcome.

This new guy had no idea the man opposite him on the street equally dressed up against the cold had once been a resident there.

A couple of things had changed though.

The booth Tomaso used to sit in had gone and been replaced by another black telephone box type version against the main outside wall of the palazzo. The old site where Inspector Drago had discovered the second body had been left open with a concrete slab covering the old man-hole.

Ronnie wondered if the new booth also had an electric fire somehow secreted within its environs?

His phone rang and he stepped into a shop doorway to receive the call.

It was Inspector Drago.

He had a proposition for him.

*

'We need to find some fingerprints of Darius Celestini,' Dom Drago mused as he sat at his desk with DS Chilabon standing arms folded in front of him. The email messages he had read from his sergeant didn't help lift his somewhat flagging spirits.

'He *may* have submitted his thumb print when he applied for a passport or driving license,' Chilabon ventured. 'I think it was mandatory then before we joined the European Union. It still might be?'

'Okay, Amanda,' Drago sat thinking before sitting up

171

straight. 'Get on to Rome and see what you can dig up. It's our only evidence he was in that taxi. He was described as wearing the fur coat the night of the murder but I haven't seen him wear one like that.'

'Is it worth getting a search warrant for his place to see if we can find it?' Chilabon enquired.

'Probably destroyed it, the cunning bastard,' Drago replied bitterly. 'Anyway I asked Signor Cabot if he had a fingerprint of his employer somewhere? He was non-committal but would have a think.'

Chilabon smiled at the inspector's cunning.

Drago then saw Station Sergeant Degrelli loitering by his office door with a furtive air, checking if the coast was clear before he could share his experience with the inspector.

He didn't want some passing station functionary ear-wigging what he was saying.

*

'Not you too?' Inspector Dom Drago remarked with more of a whisper than an exclamation of exasperation. 'You saw this figure who resembles the artist's impression of the person who was seen entering the late Contessa's apartment?'

Drago stopped there, waiting for a 'perhaps' or 'may have been mistaken,' issue from the bluff sergeant's mouth but denial came there none.

'You realise what you are saying?' Drago asked looking straight in the eye at the uncharacteristically nervous sergeant like a naughty child.

'Well, I rushed in straight away, sir,' Degrelli replied listening to himself, scarcely believing it either! 'And she was

172

gone!' he continued with open arms as if the gesture backed up his story.

'As it happens sergeant, I believe you. I am not a practising Catholic, as you are I know. However in my family there are members who every so often, particularly Sunday, offer prayer to what they cannot see but are convinced by their faith is present all around us. It is not such a big leap for us then to acknowledge that there are such other energies present beyond theirs and my comprehension. Who am I to scorn such beliefs? But the interesting question is, why Sergeant Degrelli?'

Dom Drago stopped and pondered. 'Why would the spirit visit *this* office?'

'Our boss is a practising Catholic too,' Sergeant Degrelli offered, still standing in front of the boss's desk.

'Yes, he is,' Drago said slowly, right hand on chin. 'Perhaps having been rescued from its lonely grave, it was attracted to believers who were trying to find the answers to the mystery of why she had been put there,' Drago said, thinking out loud as much as offering a considered explanation. 'Signor Ronnie Cabot also apparently saw her pointing at the ceiling in his apartment where Signor Scilaci would later vandalise and find effects from the wartime connected with the case.'

'Perhaps she knows we are looking and is watching us,' Degrelli said vaguely, before collecting himself and asking to return to his duties.

'Thank you, Sergeant,' Drago said.

'By the way, sir, how did you know I was a practising Catholic?

Inspector Drago tapped his nose.

'Know what this is? He asked.

Blank look in response.

'A copper's nose,' Bruno replied. 'Never wrong.'

'*And* you worship in San Justin's church in Pescara. My cousin too.'

Degrelli laughed out loud at Drago's knowledge and walked back to reception, closing the inspector's office door.

Nine p.m.

After lessons finished in Chieti Scalo, Ronnie walked down to the tram stop to find a note taped to the lamp-post informing commuters that due to an electrical fault, there was no service that night and he had to make his own arrangements to get home.

Cursing that he could have asked a parent of one of his students to take him part of the way home at least, he looked up and down the street, even now at just after nine at night, was almost empty with a chill wind blowing.

Deciding though it was cold, he had not walked anywhere in a long while, he determined the exercise was called for to reach his home.

Setting off at a brisk pace, he skirted round the south-west slopes of the old city via the circuitous *Via Madonna Degli Angeli* that snaked its way past picturesque villas and small shops, subsequently being slightly out of breath by the time he reach the road up the hill to the old city, a little before ten o'clock.

Ronnie, being was also a little asthmatic, had to take care with his breathing routine, nevertheless stopped to view the twinkling lights of Chieti Scalo behind him on the plains towards the coast.

Looking up at the panoramic view of the city several hundred feet above him, Ronnie stood transfixed, absorbing the Stygian landscape completely encircling the antique settlement.

The road being devoid of traffic or even people, left Cabot feeling like humanity's last representative as he continued uphill a bit more, past the little city museum situated next to the baroque single arch Pescara gate, built on the site of the Roman original when Chieti was a walled town.

Lights inside the arch's inner ceiling illuminated as well as emphasising its pale yellow-ochre colours while also throwing delicate shadows on small figurines akin to gargoyles, perched on the top ledges on either side of the towering gate.

Stopping to catch his breath again, he then continued walking at a more gentle upward gradient towards the main Corso that wound its way along the top of the ridge.

Having been educated in the classics, Ronnie couldn't help discern the distant croaking of frogs in the distance?

'Brekakex brekakex brekakex – koax koax koax!'

The froggy philharmonic from schooldays now replaying in his mind had formed the soundtrack of the Greek playwright Aristophanes' famous play he had studied in the lower sixth.

Were there frogs in Italy?

He hadn't seen any.

In *"The Frogs,"* Aristophanes makes the little beggars follow the god Dionysius in his quest into the underworld, to provide comic relief.

Ronnie had *risen* from the underworld since nine p.m. – or at least the plains of Chieti Scalo and now he had reptilian company.

Now striding along amongst hidden diners, he was not just visually enchanted by the colours of the night, his nose was being gently seduced by more pungent smells of cooking emanating from shadowy orange and beige low-rise 19th century baroque and early 20th century apartments.

Successive sirens of cooking smells enticed him over *their* threshold to savour homemade pasta, meatballs or pizza gently cooking within, but Ronnie had to keep walking to escape the bitter cold that had followed him home from work.

He turned a small corner in a narrow lane and there it was.

A full moon like a large circle of inviting parmesan cheese, just ready to drop into his lap, floated full frontal in the sky above a darkened extended silhouette of residences in a variety of architectural styles.

Little twinkling white, yellow and orange lights lit up random windows, lamp-posts and the odd street light.

The pop singer Sting's stripped down *'Moon over Bourbon Street,'* played mainly on a single cello, came into his mind, perfectly capturing his experience of traversing the narrow ancient empty streets, some of them dating back several hundred years. Even in midwinter, this collision of senses could do nothing more than navigate Cabot through living history. Never seemingly more than ten feet away from a kitchen at any one time on his progress, communing the ritual of their evening meals, Ronnie couldn't help but fantasising as he walked along, of being invited inside any one of them.

*

By the time, he reached his flat it was almost eleven o'clock but not too late for him to commune with his fellow diners, at least a tired teacher. There may have been just him at his little wooden table but putting Sting's *'The dream of the blue turtles,'* on his CD player, he could at least still make an effort. A cold beer was found lurking in the fridge along with some tasty prosciutto and some slices of fresh bread from the baker down the street, bought earlier in the day. Along with some black olives and cherry tomatoes, it was a feast fit for a king, or least a tired teacher.

177

Laying his phone on the table, he sat down in his easy chair facing his by now darkened balcony and listened quietly to the sounds, the beer for comfort.

Outside the constellation of Orion was just becoming visible in the night sky behind the old, deserted square.

Tuesday 29 February – 8.50 a.m.

A convoy of two Alfa Romeo police cars and a police Land Rover Discovery made their way out of Chieti's western suburbs downhill into the wide valley bottom towards the distant mountains that straddled the Abruzzo/Lazio border regions.

Signor Darius Celestini, his lawyer Innocente Lollis and several Carabinieri officers plus Inspector Domenico Drago were on their way to visit the Celestini family farm in the rolling hills above the Alterno-Pescara river thirty miles or so west from Chieti.

The inspector was in one of his contemplative, playful moods his subordinates admired while his critics thought it made him appear too clever by half. Indeed his little flights of fancy gave him, he thought, an edge on problem solving that left other follow-the-numbers type cops trailing.

Putting Matt Munroe singing *'On a day like this,'* that opened his favourite English language film *'The Italian Job,'* on the Land Rover CD player, he was intrigued to see Celestini's reaction to his little joke as the latter sat stone-faced in the back seat.

Did Celestini indeed *know* the film he wondered? He ran an institute that promoted English and by extension, its culture.

A similar drive through the Apennines that opened the classic British film ended in a mob hit in a mountain tunnel. Celestini, squashed in the back seat next to his round lawyer, was giving nothing away, to the wily inspector's chagrin.

179

The police cars climbed higher into the hills on hairpin bends with sheer drops on one side as the mafia character driving the orange Lamborghini had done in the aforesaid film.

Inspector Drago was not in a Lamborghini but still wondered what exactly lay ahead especially as they drove through similar mountain tunnels.

Signor Celestini had been vague about his family connections though he himself was apparently single and had no other known family. Inspector Drago however, was convinced there was more to find out.

*

Soon, Darius pointed out a tatty signpost as the convoy proceeded along a narrow sunken road having turned off the main highway some way back.

The vehicles slowed down as much because of the state of the deteriorated frosty road as the sheep who wandered around in the vicinity as roadside fences had broken down in places.

Darius then directed the little convoy up a dirt track with deep vehicle ruts a hundred yards or so to an impressive cream coloured rustic farm house with expansive albeit somewhat overgrown gardens front and back with uninterrupted views of the Apennines in the near distance.

Beige shutters had closed all the windows on both floors giving the house an ominous air as if it were collaborating with its owner to keep the curious out and preserve the secrets deemed inappropriate to share.

A young man dressed in jeans and outdoors clothes came out of what seemed like a small cottage next to the track and opened a creaky wrought iron gate, waving surreptitiously at Darius whom he spotted in the Land Rover's back seat. An old man in a rocking chair sat on a dark red coloured patio floor behind large conservatory doors.

'Who are they?' Drago asked, pointing at the two figures with his gloved left hand.

'Old Vasco and his son,' Darius responded deadpan. 'They look after the farmhouse for a few hours a day, but live in the next village.'

'Oh I see,' Drago replied giving the pensioner a quick cursory glance but not seeing much due to the flat cap pulled down most of his face.

A few yards further on and turning into a grassy yard next to the house, everyone mercifully got out of the cars and stretched their legs. Empty stable buildings formed three sides of an enclosed quad they had driven into with a large rambling barn next door.

Detailing two officers to search the farmhouse having been given the keys by Darius, retrieved from under some bricks by the front door, Drago and the rest of the group set off to a little orchard, just down a grassy path.

'This way,' Darius said as they picked their way along the overgrown path that had also turned muddy after recent thaws.

Presently they reached the orchard a hundred yards or so away with Darius opening a little wrought iron gate, just visible from the path they had just traversed. The little group then trooped in and became aware of a square flat black granite marker in the middle of several tall trees, overgrown with grass and weeds.

All moved to the black marker site and stood in a little circle, coats and hats huddled close to keep out the biting wind.

'Here is where my father sleeps,' Darius said quietly, hands

181

locked behind his back.

'There is no writing here, no dates signor,' Drago remarked looking at the blank black plaque. 'Why not?'

'Why?' Darius responded. 'No need to advertise where he lies. Only my family need to know,' he replied defensively.

'Did he change your surname or did you do it?' Drago asked, arms folded.

'He decided to, and, as soon as I was born I think he made me the legal owner of the Palazzo Gran Sasso and all his businesses, on paper at least. He knew a lot of ex-comrades in the area who helped him with the paperwork so he could stay permanently here on the farm and leave everything else to estate agents and lawyers,' Darius responded, hands in pockets with a kind of dreamlike disposition as if he thought merely being in his father's presence was a soothing balm. 'When I was eighteen, I left the farm to live in Chieti and take over running his business and then I bought the school.'

'How did a post war fascist officer live on in peace after the war, never prosecuted for his actions, raise enough money to buy the palazzo?' Drago enquired. 'The state must have known he was here. He can't have had that much money either.'

'No one bothered him, inspector. He got loans from local banks I think but everything was paid back,' Celestini replied defiantly. 'I owe no one nothing!'

'Where did you go to school then signor?' Drago persevered, dissatisfied with the answers he was getting.

'Over there in the village,' Darius pointed vaguely to an area towards the hills.

Everyone looked towards where he was pointing.

No one could see any buildings, least of all a school.

'So your name would appear in the school records signor?

Drago enquired.

'Of course,' Darius replied shrugging.

'Your mother signor?' Drago enquired.

Mountain winds then blew up strong gusts ending any further dialogue so the freezing group turned and made their way back towards the farmhouse.

'Signor Celestini,' Inspector Drago said irritated as much by the cold as the uncooperative witness in front of him, turned to him as they both got back into the back of the car and the police driver in the front. 'I know it was you were involved in Ella Frantoni's murder but I can't prove it yet! The papers say she was allegedly providing covert information to the police department from the Comune and this for some reason was a threat to you. Is that why you visited the party secretary during the day recently? You felt threatened by what Ella was doing poking around in your business affairs? Decided she needed to be removed huh?'

'Prove it, inspector,' Darius said quietly between gritted teeth, shivering and pulling his expensive leather gloves tight around his fingers. 'It's all lies.'

'You must stop bothering my client now,' lawyer Lollis chipped in, having got into the front passenger seat and cowering in his greatcoat. 'He's shown you where his father is buried and as far as I can see you have no hard evidence of anything! Supposition inspector,' Lollis said, turning back round in the passenger seat to watch the road ahead home.

'I haven't forgotten you breaking into that young girl's student room,' Drago said ignoring the lawyer and pointing his gloved finger at Celestini, 'but I will make it my business to put you away, you can count on that! Investigations will continue so the Prosecutor will ultimately decide. Meantime, don't leave the country and you will surrender your passport to my officer who

183

will accompany you back to your apartment in Termoli for that purpose. By the way who is your next of kin?'

'Do I have to answer that?' Darius enquired.

'No signor, but it would be suspicious if you didn't, wouldn't it?'

'Then I am declining to answer,' Darius responded with a shrug.

'I see,' Drago replied looking back to the lonely little orchard, swaying under buffets of mountain wind, 'then I shall assume you have something to hide.'

'Think what you like,' Darius responded sullenly.

*

There was no more to be done there as winter shoved its icy blasts up the valley. Inspector Drago and the little convoy headed for home. Nothing of interest had been found in the empty farmhouse other that it had evidently not been lived in for some years. There wasn't even a phone connection.

The convey carefully set off down the track whence they had come, Drago noticing that though the younger man closed the gate after the convoy had left, the elderly rocker was now absent.

'He has probably gone home,' Darius volunteered, reading the inspector's probing mind. 'Ennio will follow him.'

'I see,' came the muffled response from the inspector, not really seeing anything.

*

Several hours later and true to Inspector Drago's word, Officer Castello, accompanying Darius to his villa in Termoli had acquired Celestini's passport.

Castello had been asked on the quiet to see if he could see a heavy fur coat anywhere in Celestini's property. As it was not an official search, Castello could not actually *search* the place but the inspector was interested in what the policeman might find. Castello made an excuse to go to Celestini's toilet at the back of the apartment so as he wandered down, his eyes looked at any visible coat hook or surface where clothes may be.

Nothing.

If Celestini had had it here, it had probably gone, Castello subsequently reported back to his boss later in the day.

The language school proprietor was now formally released back into a grateful learning community.

*

Inspector Drago sat tetchily at Bruno's desk at police headquarters. All roads led to Darius Celestini as the murderer but he couldn't get that final piece of evidence.

The kindling was round the bonfire under Celestini but Drago had no matches.

Would it change Celestini's actions now, knowing he was the main suspect in the Frantoni murder? The only suspect?

The inspector considered putting a tail on him or even tapping his phone but realised in a small town like Chieti, it would never work. Celestini would be on his guard now.

Everyone knew everyone including police and the resident criminality.

*

It was just after six o'clock when Ronnie slowly sat down in his easy chair in the little sitting room overlooking the piazza as he tried to take in Darius' deadpan news delivered down the phone.

No more English lessons were being offered at the Comune with immediate effect. It seemed the investigation into Ella Frantoni's death was drawing too much negative light on the Christian Liberal Party so headquarters in Rome had withdrawn funding for English lessons. Immediately Ronnie thought of the bottom line, his more than Darius'. They would both face loss of earnings.

Cabot wasn't very happy to stay in Chieti even rent-free if he were earning less.

Darius promised Cabot he was onto it and would see what he could find to make up Ronnie's earnings – preferably thrice-weekly sessions of six hours in total would be ideal.

Ronnie however, doubted Darius in his present distracted state of mind with a police enquiry would be able to find him more work. He decided therefore to put his coat on and take the tram down to Chieti Scalo station to see Bernardo, his English student and its railway station manager. Bernardo did night shifts on alternate weeks so Ronnie knew he would be on duty now.

He thought of calling Anna to see what she was doing but after finishing his *pizza-a-taglio* from a little fast-food outlet on the square, he just didn't feel in the mood. If she wanted to see him she could bloody well call him for a change.

*

Sharing local bottled beer with Bernardo in his back office while listening to the Alan Parson's Project, *'The turn of a friendly*

186

card,' in particular was a pleasant way of passing time for both of them. Bernardo practised his English and Ronnie had a go at Italian. He also introduced Bernardo to Joe Jackson, a favourite of Cabot's. Jackson's *'Body and Soul'* album of sublime musical quality and atmosphere, Tom felt sure would resonate with his fellow musical *compadre*.

The railway company, to Cabot's surprise, didn't seem to mind both of them having a quiet beer while listening to their favourite tunes in the manager's office while their manager was supposed to be on duty. Ronnie wasn't objecting though Bernardo read his mind.

'The company don't mind while the station is quiet like it is now,' he said putting his beer can down with a faraway look in his eyes.

'Most people don't want to do night shift anyway.'

'Graveyard shift, we say in England, which caused Bernardo much mirth. 'Tell the company you are having a private English lesson so you can keep up with European railway magazines! Why not?' Bernardo laughed as he sat opposite his English teacher in the only other office chair next to an opaque glass window that fronted the main line platform on the other side.

Bernardo ran out of steam trying to laugh along with his teacher. Cabot knew what the problem was, as usual.

'Are your girls giving you grief again?'

Bernardo shrugged. 'I am a man. What do I know how girls think or how to treat them, especially teenage ones? If only their mother had stayed,' he said, sadly folding his arms.

'It's just a phase they are going through – teenagers,' and here Ronnie indicated with his beer can, the language school down the street, 'can be stroppy and confrontational. You just have to keep your cool,' he said. 'But, I don't live with them like

187

you do!' he finished up with a half laugh.

A pause as both contemplated the music while finishing off their bottled beers.

'Do you think Signor Celestini will find you more work?' he asked. 'Here,' whispered Bernardo loudly, leaning forward on his desk and pointing his index finger at the floor oblivious to anyone else listening in the deserted outside corridor, 'there are, how you say pyramids. *Hierarchies* of people in power but also there are people who move effortlessly between these 'pyramids' but this movement is in the shadows.

The Christian Liberal Party is a political party as you know, but made up of people who also exist in other pyramids – businessmen for example like your employer. You never know which pyramid, property development, finance, security and criminality yes, that too, they are *lurking in* at any one point. Where there is an opportunity, these types of men are there,' Bernardo said cynically while checking his online Italian/English dictionary. 'Look at me. I am a station manager and have a senior position but because I am not a political party member, I remain just that. I am also a divorcee which our Catholic church disapprove of. But,' and here he leaned back and smiled, 'if I were a member of the church, a political party member and from an old established family I would be *someone* with a car, secretary and town house,' he said laughing with his open arms.

'And decent girlfriend!' provoked Ronnie, causing much mirth on both sides. 'Well, I am an outsider and a Protestant and you are a father who's doing his best for his family!' Cabot continued, smiling as Bernardo made a mock crucifix in front of him.

Ronnie liked Bernardo because he was easy to talk to, just trying to raise his daughters and have a decent life. He wasn't ripping off the EU for subsidies like Cabot's Christian Liberal Party students claimed to be doing. Bernardo described himself as an honest man which made his loyalties not for sale, much like fellow travellers Inspectors Drago and Bruno presumably, Cabot concluded.

Suddenly, Ronnie's feelings about the mateyness of Signor Orazio at the Comune seemed hollow and not worth for him, developing.

Would political people like these have your back covered in an emergency?

Wednesday 1 March – Eight a.m.

There it was on the morning TV news.

The revelation that Darius' father had been identified as a wartime fascist commander who had acquired the Palazzo Gran Sasso at some point post war after the previous owners were supposed to have fled. The father had previously used a top floor apartment to fire at passers-by in the main street below and then allegedly, the TV news said, to bury two anti-fascist soldiers he had murdered using a concealed pistol while they were guarding him after he had been taken prisoner. One body had been discovered by accident during building work to install a new boiler, the reporter said. The other had been found by police who eventually found the hidden man-hole where it had been deposited.

Signor Darius Celestini had not played a part in these crimes as they had obviously occurred before he was born but was being investigated in connection with the murder of a secretary at the Comune. Subsequently he had been released pending further investigations, the reporter informed the viewers.

'Unbelievable,' Ronnie couldn't help repeating as he almost dropped his cheese on toast on the living room floor, his eyes riveted on the TV report.

The reporter didn't mention Signor Tomaso Scilaci or the unexplained death of the Contessa though which was just as intriguing.

A few minutes later, his mobile rang.

It was Inspector Drago.

'Hi, Signor Cabot,'

Inspector Drago started with easy pleasantries before Ronnie managed to interrupt, 'I've just seen the news report. It's incredible really and the report doesn't even mention the Contessa or the old caretaker.'

'No,' Drago conceded but I am keeping an open mind on the old lady's death for now. Looks like the caretaker was right about Darius' family being involved in the killings but as the suspected wartime murderer is apparently now dead, that part of the case is closed. I wanted to tell you that the two bodies that were found at Palazzo Gran Sasso are going to be reburied at Sangro River War Cemetery. Sorry for short notice but would you like to attend the ceremony and a small wake afterwards?

'Yes, I would like to very much,' Ronnie replied.

'Signor Tomaso Scilaci's family will also attend. I'll send a car to your apartment for you on tomorrow lunchtime. Signor Celestini was also invited but don't know if he will come.'

Darius had probably been persuaded by Drago as Darius later texted Cabot to say he would pay him in lieu while he was attending the funeral. Darius himself wouldn't be attending, Cabot was informed.

Ronnie also wondered if Anna would attend but didn't want to text her about it.

He would just see.

Thursday 2 March – Nine a.m.

On a cold sharp morning, a light blue and white police car and driver was transporting Ronnie Cabot as the sole passenger to the Sangro River War Cemetery roughly twenty-five miles south east of Chieti. He had put a jacket and tie on and brought his camera for some vague reason of recording his attendance and a few snaps to remember the occasion by.

After about an hour, negotiating the frosty Contrada Sentinella highway as it twisted through small villages and round hills covered with an early morning dusting of powdery snow, Cabot's police car finally arrived at the cemetery.

Getting out and pulling his winter coat closer around him, Ronnie and his Carabinieri driver walked across the circular expanse of neat white headstones to a little grouping on the far side next to two open graves.

The wind swirled and eddied around the grave stones creating a curious whistling sound as the few trees on the outer edge gently swayed in the winter gusts. He nodded a greeting to a wrapped-up Inspector Drago and…

…there she was.

Anna wrapped up in her pink winter coat and pink woollen hat with her wrapped up parents and twitchy looking uncle, plus other relatives and friends of the family presumably. At least he knew *her* and waved as he stood the other side of the open grave near the priest.

Two light brown closed coffins were positioned by two open

graves. They were draped in the Italian flag and a matching set of what Cabot presumed were military medals. Both coffins were being blessed by the priest as he splashed holy water on each as Ronnie approached the little gathering.

The whole process was easy for Ronnie to follow even though it was in Italian and mercifully not over long so everyone could get out of the freezing cold. He was pleased for Anna, Tomaso and their family that now, Margaretta Embriaco, whose restless spirit had seemingly manifested herself to him in his old bedroom may now have partial *'justice'* in lying with her other fallen comrades. Testalardi Maglio the other martyred soldier however, had gone to his grave without any relatives to acknowledge the fact, though the priest had ensured that both would be received by a loving God in the next world.

*

Later, as the relatives and friends were sat down to dinner in a nearby restaurant especially booked and paid for by the government, Ronnie managed to sit next to Anna, the ensuing public general conversation between them ironing over such recriminations of why one hadn't called the other about attending. Their friendship could therefore continue while the noise of waiters serving plates of pasta and local wines continued noisily all around them. Ronnie would have preferred they all went away and there was just her there. In spite of everything they resolved to meet up again the following weekend in Pescara city centre and to confirm times by texting.

*

'What happened to my sister you bastard?' the pale man in his thirties dressed in a long dark coat and beanie stepped out from behind the lit concrete pillar in the Comune underground car park.

'How did you get in here?' the Christian Liberal Party Secretary stepped back in surprise, looking around to see if anyone could step in and help him.

No one on hand to provide respite for the jobbing politician.

'You were her boss!' the interloper continued pointing his finger aggressively at the secretary's nose, his emotions threatening to get the better of him.

Cesare Frantoni was a successful architect with a practice in Pescara so when he realised the investigation into his sister's murder was going nowhere, decided by himself to up the ante.

'The police are investigating so it's up them. Now leave me alone!' Orazio Mancetti struggled to get away from the intruder's menacing stance and reach his car a few steps away.

'I blame you, you piece of...' Frantoni shouted as just then two other employers of the Comune appeared in the car park area.

Frantoni slunk away, making veiled threats as Mancetti quickly got into his car and screeched away up the ramp to the street outside.

Party Secretary Mancetti was on his phone immediately, dialling Domenico Drago's personal number, as given to him after the recent murder of one of his secretaries.

'Inspector? I have been threatened by this lunatic Frantoni who blames me for his sister's death and confronted me just now in the Comune car park.'

'Signor Mancetti,' Bruno replied in a restrained tone, 'You have hardly cooperated with my investigation. I asked you if internal calls are monitored or the precise duties Signorina Ella had been carrying out at the time of her death but you haven't got back to me on either which makes me think you may have something to hide. Do I need to get official permission from Rome to investigate your internal and external phone lines and records at the Comune?' I can get it sir.'

'It's hard to give a proper answer,' Mancetti said defensively as he drove along the road home. 'The technology we have is confusing and outdated but I have asked the Comune if they can update it and provide some kind of technical information on the communication capabilities. I certainly don't like being confronted in a car park that's supposed to be secure.'

'What can I do about that?' Drago asked though he wasn't really surprised. Which public car park round here was?

'Find him and warn him off?' came the angry response.

'Maybe,' Drago responded, 'but people like you need to be seen to be cooperating with the police so people like our Signor Frantoni can be reassured. Were you connected to Ella Frantoni's death?' Drago asked speculatively.

'Definitely not!' Mancetti shouted into the phone before finishing the call.

*

No sooner had Inspector Drago been cut off with a shouty curt order by Signor Orazio Mancetti, he recognised an incoming call from Deputy Director General Nerone on the phone console on his desk.

'He'll be wanting a positive update on the case, no doubt about that,' Drago sighed, his heart already sinking.

Any time of day a call like this to a police station however it was dressed up, invariably meant pressure from the most senior policeman in the Abruzzo region.

A man who also happened to be an occasional golfing partner of Darius Celestini amongst other men of means in the area. Why not? It wasn't against the law.

The ensuing conversation was the police Deputy Director mostly talking and the inspector mostly listening with frequent interspersions of 'Yes sir.'

The decision had been made and Inspector Domenico Drago was being transferred back to his Rome headquarters and Inspector Giordano Bruno reassuming his role.

The higher-ups obviously were uncomfortable with what he, Inspector Drago was doing exposing corruption and possible criminal behaviour in collusion with the local branch of a national political party. Now Inspector Giordano Bruno was taking over again. Unlike his historical namesake he probably wouldn't be burnt at the stake, though possibly Bruno might be shown one with Darius Celestini's finger prints on the kindling.

*

2.05 p.m.

'Looks like I am going back to Rome then. The criminal fraternity there have had their holiday,' Drago's grim sarcasm down the phone was his attempt to lift his fellow inspector's spirits.

'I heard,' Jordi Bruno replied with a brief laugh. 'Commissioner Nerone rang to tell me I too am going back to work though he understands I have suffered a grievous loss.'

'I wish I could have resolved this awful situation by now,' Drago continued, sighing. 'But, I think there are those in power here who want to leave things as they are for now and it seems our esteemed police commissioner is one of them.' Then, changing tack, 'How are you now?'

A pause.

'I don't trust the Comune pen-pushers starting with the Christian Liberal Party Secretary downwards,' Jordi Bruno replied bitterly and honestly with his close friend. 'Ella was a threat to them,' he continued. 'But, what will Nerone do then? Close the investigation? I ask myself who benefits?' he said snorting down the phone.

'Well, her brother Cesare is convinced the party secretary was involved in her murder. Maybe even gave the word,' Drago commented quietly. 'I think he watches too many news reports but I have no proof that would stand up in court. I have been waiting for a sample, if it exists, of Signor Celestini's finger prints but so far I have heard nothing from Rome. Without a confession as well really, I am stuck,' Drago sighed again, 'and no one is confessing!'

'I know what I will do first thing I am back. Bring in that senior secretary Ceresa and question her,' Bruno replied. 'If anyone knows what happened to Ella, she will.'

'Well, before I go back to my own happy hunting ground I will go see our architect friend Cesare Frantoni at his office,'

'Why not?' Bruno replied. 'Rattle his cage a bit.'

'Good luck and don't forget,' Justice takes us to strange places sometimes even to the world beyond,' Drago continued. 'Your namesake laid down his life for truth. I think neither of us should shy away from doing something similar?'

Friday 3 March – 10.03 a.m.

On his way to talk to Cesare Frantoni at his Pescara place of work, Inspector Drago took a call on his mobile phone.

Signor Giacomo Lettieri the national secretary of the Christian Liberal Party was calling from headquarters in Rome.

And he wasn't happy either.

Before Drago could even get a word in, a long stream of complaints ensued about some lunatic called Frantoni who was threatening the local branch secretary in Chieti and where was the police protection?

'Police protection? Give me a break, sir,' Inspector Drago replied finally managing to get a word in edgeways.

More veiled threats about taking Drago off the case caused him to pull in off the road so he could talk to this idiot who spoke in long sentences without punctuation.

'How did you get my personal number Signor Lettieri?' Drago asked.

'The Christian Liberal party has access to such numbers that can be used in an emergency,' came the vague reply.

'Is this such an emergency? I think not. I don't even work in Chieti any more now,' Drago replied, his anger rising. I don't know what strings you pulled but…'

'Signor Mancetti would value protection!' Lettieri broke in.

'Why?'

'That dead bitch's brother!' he shouted back.

'Sir!' Drago replied angrily. 'This is disrespectful language to the murder victim. If you or your department have information on Ella Frantoni's death you should share it okay? No go away or I will take up your threats with the police commissioner!'

He then ended the call.

He doubted this preening pen-pusher on the other side of the Apennines had taken in the fact that he had been recalled to Rome anyway and that Inspector Bruno was now in charge again.

*

Inspector Drago, still irritated from his previous phone call, arrived outside the prestigious architectural practice in an upmarket suburb with high walls and buzzers on the imposing faceless front doors.

Finally, let in after announcing his name and who he wanted to speak to, he climbed some outside marble stairs and gained entrance to a large airy modern office.

Not entirely pleased to see him, Signor Cesare Frantoni put both hands on the side of his desk.

'Turns out my sister was seeing a cop inspector! Didn't he realise he was putting her in danger?'

'I don't think your late sister saw it like that sir,' Drago said quietly, sticking up for his fellow inspector.

Not succeeding so far.

'You think so?' Frantoni continued. 'I,' and here he pointed to his chest, 'would have told her to run a mile! She's dead now so you tell me there's no connection?'

'I hear what you're saying sir but sadly the past is done. I can't say if there's a connection but I assure you my colleague Inspector Bruno shall find out who killed your sister. He is tenecious and has an able team working for him. Now, sir,' Drago continued following Frantoni over to his desk and sitting down in front of the metal and glass table. 'I am here in connection with the recent altercation between you and Signor Mancetti?'

Drago then accepted an offer of an espresso from a secretary entering the room after hearing the raised voices. Somewhat sullenly Frantoni asked her to bring in two.

'What were you doing in the Comune basement car park Signor Frantoni? Drago asked him after sipping his espresso a few minutes later. 'I could arrest you for trespass.'

'It was a public car park,' Frantoni replied defensively. 'I don't see any signs saying it was private. Anyway I know that Mancetti from TV – he's all smiles and *bonhomie* but he's a slippery bastard and has fingers in many pies.'

'Your evidence? Your sister?'

'We talked a bit,' Frantoni replied, and that was the extent of his intelligence gained. 'But, never on the phone inspector. We knew it could be tapped. I think the internal phones were too, illegally mind,' Frantoni said pointing his well-manicured finger in Drago's direction. 'That's how they knew who my sister was talking to.'

'The municipality tapping their own phones from the inside is illegal obviously,' Inspector Drago replied.

'Mancetti's the main man. He had to know about it,' Frantoni continued. 'I have no proof but I expect the police department to get on with it and shit on that Mancetti's head. He deserves it,' Frantoni replied, arms folded sitting back on the opposite office chair.

'Well, my colleague Inspector Bruno is returning to work and he will catch those responsible for your sister's death,' Drago replied finishing up 'but my advice to you Signor Frantoni is to stay away from the Comune and let the police do their duty.'

Late Afternoon

As soon as Jordi Bruno was back in his old familiar leather seat in his office in Chieti police station, he put in a call to Domenico Drago back in *his* office in Rome after a hectic helicopter ride back. Pleasantries were exchanged and not just on the superficial level.

Being close colleagues now, Inspector Drago was inevitably sad and frustrated that Ella Frantoni's murderer was still walking around.

'Apart from breaking into his office there isn't much else I can do to get a sample of Signor Celestini's finger prints,' Bruno laughed with a bitter undercurrent. 'I gather Signor Cabot was approached discreetly to see if he can help but short of following his boss around, it wasn't really viable.'

'I looked at CCTV at several points on the route Ella took but found nothing useful that could definitely put him on the scene,' Drago continued. 'But Celestini knows the police are onto him and will tread carefully I am sure.'

'Good,' Bruno responded, leaning back in his chair. 'I want to see him sweat.'

'Celestini said he was driving down to Vasto in his Mercedes the evening of Ella's murder but we couldn't find him on CCTV for the highway because, obviously, he wasn't there in the first place. He was driving that Volvo from Chieti following Ella's car but I couldn't prove it.'

'It's a flimsy case I can see,' Bruno replied 'but Celestini can be sure I won't be giving up. I will nail that bastard.' Then, 'by the way the late Contessa's DNA sample arrived on my desk. You requested it?'

'Yes,' Drago replied. 'It may be significant.'

'I have every confidence,' Jordi Bruno replied, reading the departing inspector's comments in an accompanying note.

*

Ronnie Cabot was having his weekly evening English lesson with trainee doctors in Chieti Scalo health centre, five minutes down the road from the language centre on the main road where he was normally based.

Because there was a popular pastry shop next to the health centre, he invariably found one of his trainee medic students buying their home-made Croissants all made to order, ready to eat during a break in the lesson.

When he had first arrived in Italy several months ago, Ronnie had taken on board all the guidebook stories of how healthy the diet was and the near all year-round outdoor lifestyle. The diet was indeed better than anything he had previously come across living in England, but Chieti, being on a fairly steep hill suffered with great snowfalls and black ice in winter. The friendliness of most people too was as it had been written about, especially in a smallish town like Chieti where there were few native English speakers. Local food and drink specialities, how they were prepared and served was the stuff of the Sunday colour supplements back in the UK as well as in Italy.

However, the longer Ronnie lived in Chieti, the more he realised there was an uncomfortable side to the society he had lived in relatively freely up to then, though Darius Celestini had only just given him his official residence permit after seven months of asking.

The trainee doctor students had informed Cabot almost to a man and woman, that none of them paid taxes on their full-time earnings, for reasons he could never really understand from a financial, let alone a moral standpoint. They were all guaranteed jobs for life by the state with a generous pension, but when Cabot tried hesitatingly to venture that Italy would eventually have to pay the price for this cavalier attitude to money, however far away in the future, he was greeted with derision and laughter; he was just a foreigner so what did he know?

As with other students of his, in particular his well turned out AGIP petrol company executives, the well turned-out doctors Ronnie taught didn't shop at UPIM, the mid-range department store on the Corso where Ronnie bought most of his clobber.

A committed Brexiter, having voted 'No' in Cameron's 2016 referendum, Ronnie had frequently sighed to himself finding out how much EU money was used to prop up large scale tax evasion hereabouts. Italy and German bank loans he was told, were always ready apparently to bail the state out.

He had already been told by Signor Orazio Mancetti at the Christian Liberal branch offices where he had taught that they too deceived central government, oblivious of the fact that as self-proclaimed neo-fascists hiding under a 'Liberal' umbrella, they were taking advantage (albeit a tiny part) of Ronnie's taxes.

He couldn't, however, fault the medical students' enthusiasm to learn English.

If there had been a bar on their premises like at the Comune, he would have been in the bar with most of them after lessons until the wee hours. Just as well then probably, he waved goodbye to his keen learners after late night pastries, in time to catch the last tram up the hill to his flat in Chieti.

For the umpteenth time, he concluded he was a guest and had to take the local population as he found them. Their values and outlook on life were in the main the same as Ronnie's though on occasion they jarred against each other somewhat.

Monday 6 March – 8.18 a.m.

True to his word, Inspector Giordano Bruno took up the reins of Ella's murder investigation, ably initiated by Inspector Drago, immediately on arrival at work that morning. Calling in DS Chilabon, she was instructed to take one other police officer and go round to the Comune to pick up Signora Ceresa for questioning.

Bruno was then on the phone to Constable Carboni ordering him to chase up any information on documentation of the alleged new Volvo owner, requested from the central records bureau in Rome. He also reminded Station Sergeant Degrelli who had walked into Bruno's office, to keep pressing Rome for any stored example of Darius' fingerprints.

Degrelli stood fidgeting in front of Bruno's desk.

'What is it Sergeant?' Bruno asked finally.

'That woman in the photo,' Degrelli said, pointing at the head and shoulders photo originally supplied by Cabot's girlfriend Anna Bianchi and now attached to the whiteboard on the opposite side of the room to the seated inspector. 'She was here, I saw her come into this office the other day,' he replied awkwardly, looking at the inspector.

If Degrelli expected a derisory laugh from his boss, he was pleasantly mistaken.

A silence descended on the office as both men thought through the implications however uncomfortable.

Jordi Bruno had already heard about paranormal activities

connected to this case – Ronnie Cabot had told him about his ghostly encounter with the woman, as had the old cleaner Violetta Crimosa. Ronnie had also told Bruno the late Contessa believed Celestini had known about the concealed body, the implication Ronnie had drawn was maybe Celestini had seen the same phantom within the Palazzo Gran Sasso. Celestini would never admit that of course.

'Okay, Sergeant, I believe you,' Inspector Bruno finally replied, sighing. 'Let's hope her burial in the war cemetery has brought peace to her soul at least.'

Sergeant Degrelli, in some slight surprise that his boss had taken all he said on board without any clarification, retreated back to his station seeing police work hereafter, in a new psychological light.

*

An hour later, Signora Michele Ceresa noticeably ill at ease and looking around at, for her, threatening surroundings, was ushered in an interview room at Chieti police station. Her lawyer, the ever-available Innocente Lollis was already sat down, note book open.

'Signora,' Inspector Bruno reminded her quietly when everyone was sat down, 'if you have any intention of deceiving us, it is a waste of time, so we…'

'No one intends deception here inspector,' Lollis piped up straight away. 'Signora Ceresa is here to fully cooperate with the police.'

'Good,' Bruno replied, sat up straight, elbows on the table, hands clasped under his chin. 'Tell me about how incoming and outgoing phone calls are monitored at the Comune.'

'I... I,' Ceresa started, looking at Lollis who smiled urbanely.

'Come, come, Signora,' Bruno continued. 'I can send in telephone engineers to check landlines and switchboards but I suspect mobile phone calls fall into the same category. I just want to know what your knowledge of Comune phone traffic is?'

'I have no knowledge of such activities. I am a regional government secretary,' she whispered.

'No!' Bruno shouted emphatically, getting out of his chair. 'You have worked there for many years and know the inner workings of local administration so that will not do!'

'Inspector, you are harassing my client!' Lollis intervened, putting his right hand on her left arm for support.

'I am not here to be pissed about!' Bruno responded walking round to the back of Ceresa's chair. 'An innocent woman working at the Comune was murdered,' he continued face down level with Ceresa's left ear.

'Inspector, your language please!' Lollis intervened, also standing up.

'You're right,' Bruno said, collecting himself and resuming his more professional demeanour. 'I am sorry.'

He needed to be calm and plot his questioning carefully.

Constable Vivante, a somewhat rotund though loyal officer was standing guard at the interview room door. Would he have intervened on Lollis' behalf to restrain an overwrought inspector?

Jordi Bruno dearly wanted to say, 'my innocent *girlfriend* was murdered,' but realised that would completely undermine his case and have Lollis complaining about conflict of interest.

The tall policeman moved back to his chair opposite the Signora and sat down.

'I am sorry about that poor woman,' Signora Ceresa replied,

dropping her mask of impassivity. 'She was my friend. I was asked to check any outside phone numbers called from the municipality and who was being called. I didn't ask why?' she responded lamely.

'Who asked you?' Bruno said quietly resuming his seat.

'I can't say inspector,' Ceresa wavered somewhat, sighing and looking at Lollis.

'Give me something to go on signora or I am going to make your life uncomfortable.'

Ceresa and Lollis conferred in whispers before she turned to the stern-faced policeman.

'If I give you a tip, will you leave me alone?' she asked, her shoulders visibly sagging.

Bruno sat up, extending his chin.

*

Before she left the station, Signora Ceresa detailed the Comune's anxiety that the interests of their members were being investigated by outside bodies (the police or the tax office for example?) and the party secretary instructed all assistant party secretaries to be wary of who contacted whom externally and what was said, if possible. A review of outside calls showed Signora Ella Frantoni had been calling this very police station on a landline though didn't know the nature of the call.

She was then asked to sign the statement to the effect and allowed to go.

Bruno was smiling all the way back to his office.

He called DS Chilabon to his office. 'Get your coat Amanda.'

'Why sir?' she asked.

'We're going on a little fishing trip courtesy of Signora Ceresa.'

*

<u>6.04 p.m.</u>

The sombre atmosphere was evident as soon as Ronnie stepped into the Chieti Scalo school reception.

Tiziana sat behind her desk, arms folded staring at the opposite skirting board; her appearance betraying degrees of anger and frustration, unusual for someone of Tiziana's eminently sensible world view.

She didn't even look up when Ronnie stopped by her desk.

This *was* unusual.

His cheery hello received no response.

'You don't know?' she asked without looking up without smiling.

'No?'

'Darius is closing the Chieti Scalo school and just keeping the school on the Corso open,' she replied sighing.

'What?' Ronnie was shocked at the news. He had no idea. 'Why?'

'No reason I can see,' she said still not moving.

'It must be connected to what was found at the palazzo, I suppose.'

'I wish nothing had been found and we could continue with our lives,' she moaned at the wall.

Was she blaming him Ronnie wondered?

It wasn't his fault there were secrets uncovered in their employer's life. Ronnie was more concerned about his next move? With the end of lessons at the Comune and no classes in

Chieti Scalo apart from the medical students, the guaranteed minimum salary per week Darius had given him regardless of his actual hours worked was staring at him now. He would have to talk with his employer as soon as possible about needing to earn more money.

Ronnie's class of mixed teenage English students were remarkably sanguine about the class possibly ending, upon hearing the news. Being in the main, unwilling learners and sent by their parents, any ray of light which meant they could study a bit less was to be embraced.

English a world language?

Not in the world of Chieti Scalo's stroppy teenagers.

'What's it got to do with me?' was their collective response.

Ronnie bade Tiziana an awkward goodnight as he left the building at the end of his classes. It was quite a cushy deal for her, he mused. She didn't have to do much except answer the phone and take payments for classes. No one bothered her there and she could watch the TV set up for the students in the reception area. She might not get such an easy number in future employment but it really wasn't his fault, he decided.

*

He called Anna who sounded flustered, too busy with studying and exams. Deciding to leave her to it he said he would text her at the end of the week and left it at that.

*

Signor Orazio was waiting for Signora Cesera when she walked back into the Comune building with a sullen air, barely able to

210

converse with security at the gate.

Their eyes met in the lobby with him motioning to her to follow him into a small ground floor office.

They were barely in the door when Mancetti closed the door behind her before roughly taking hold of her left arm to force her to face him.

'Well?' he asked six inches from her face.

'I didn't say anything,' she replied aggressively forcing him to let go of her arm and her sitting on a chair, arms crossed, lips pursed.

'I don't want that dam cop sniffing round here again. I don't want him sniffing round the party treasury books or the Comune phone lines.'

'They have no evidence for anything, trust me,' she said beginning to weary of all the subterfuge. 'That bloody Celestini, he's caused all this,' she said looking at her manager. 'Why don't you cut him off from the party?'

'He's an important man,' Mancetti said quietly. 'He is a big donor to the party.' He didn't mention to Signora Ceresa that Celestini and him were also linked via the Masonic Lodge. She didn't need to know that.

'Okay off you go and sorry for grabbing you,' he said opening the door for her.

Ceresa left without a word and without looking at her boss, almost holding onto the door handle for support.

He went downstairs immediately to the basement where the cars were parked and nodding to the guard on duty, unlocked his car and got inside.

He needed to call *his* boss.

It was a strained call to party headquarters in Rome. Complaints that the Chieti branch were being intimidated by the police were brushed off by headquarters telling Mancetti that as he had created this mess, it was up to him to sort it out. What did he want Rome to do? Realistically?

Mancetti had no real answer so his whining and complaining spent, he ended the call and sat in his car, more despondent than ever. If only they could get rid of the brother in some way, the police could be safely ignored as there was no evidence against him or his associate that could win a prosecution.

Sighing, he slowly got out of his car and trudged back upstairs to party offices.

He had barely closed his office door when he heard a commotion in the main reception area of the Comune.

Opening his door and gazing over the stone balustrade into the grand reception area, he was greeted by the sight of Inspector Bruno and his detective sergeant standing in front of the main desk.

*

'Well, well,' Jordi Bruno exclaimed as he unlocked the door to the Comune's cavernous basement.

'It's enormous,' DS Chilabon said as they stepped into a small reception area and were confronted with row upon row of dusty heavy wooden shelves filled with files, books and old-fashioned ledgers. 'What are we looking for sir?' she asked with a hint of desperation.

Jordi Bruno tapped his nose with his index finger.

Behind them in the entrance way stood two of the Comune secretaries along with several local government functionaries, curious to see what Chieti's top cop was doing there and what on earth he expected to find?

212

Among them was a strangely quiet Orazio Mancetti.

Signora Ceresa was nowhere to be seen.

Mancetti pursed lips betrayed the idea bouncing around in his brain what the bastard cop was after.

Soon enough, with the door wedged open and Bruno summoning a trolley from upstairs, he and Chilabon sat on two wooden chairs and stared at the shelves with faded labels recording decades old business and property transactions.

'Signorina Ella Frantoni was down here looking for something connected to the palazzo but what?' Bruno wondered aloud as he got up nonchalantly to scan dusty file titles connected to the Palazzo Gran Sasso stored on a nearby shelf.

'You can all go now,' he added, brushing away the little group of onlookers with a wave of his languid hand.

Mancetti was getting redder and redder in the face as he turned and stormed off.

*

Nearly half an hour later, both officers were ready to go, having been unable to unearth the clue Signora Ceresa had offered up to the inspector.

And the clue which may have got Ella murdered.

Bruno led the way slowly back to the basement entrance wondering if he had been tricked when a brilliance of light caught his attention.

The twinkling little circle of light high up on Bruno's right had been caused, on closer inspection, by a thin sunbeam shining through a corroded narrow grille letting in a degree of outside air.

'What have we here Amanda?' he asked out loud as he stopped in his tracks, picked up a chair and put it next to the partially door.

'What is it sir?' she asked as her boss gingerly got onto the chair and peered ahead of him into a gloom of cobwebs and dust.

'There's only a security camera up here, trained to cover the way into the basement,' Drago said snorting. 'The lens happened to catch the sunshine as we were walking past!'

'Lucky we didn't come on a cloudy day then sir?' DS Chilabon replied with a grave air. 'We'd never have seen it!'

'Who would want to know the comings and goings in the basement then Mandy? Bruno asked the little camera pointed directly at the door threshold taking care not to touch it. 'Call the forensic unit and get a couple of technicians here to dismantle it and bring it to the lab and a couple of uniforms to come and guard it in case it goes walkabout while we are not here!'

Wednesday 7 March – Seven Thirty a.m.

'Come in here Amanda, please?' Inspector Bruno shouted through the open office door as the in-house waiter simultaneously arrived with two fresh croissants.

Detective Sergeant Chilabon, email print off in hand, smiled a grim expression, scuffing her slight dash of lipstick.

At least, the espresso in Jordi Bruno's mouth had a pleasing creamy taste.

'The records say the Volvo has been scrapped!' Chilabon presented Bruno with the response she had received from vehicle records in Rome and driver records in Milan. 'Nearly four months ago.'

'That can't be right,' Bruno said tersely looking at Chilabon's email. 'It's sitting in the pound now!'

'I know sir,' Chilabon said, at a loss to explain. 'All I can say is obviously there is a discrepancy. It could be a question of number plates but we don't have one.'

'Well, get the car pound to check the engine block numbers. That will tell us if it is the car we are interested in okay?' Bruno said, sitting back and folding his arms, 'I would like to know how much Signor Celestini has to do with this car fraud?'

DS Chilabon stood still in front of Bruno's desk as if she were about to say something but he did it for her. 'What else?'

'We can't find any copies of Signor Celestini's fingerprints,' she said with a sigh.

'This man and his helpers have covered their tracks

215

meticulously,' Bruno said, picking up the phone and called in the police station waiter to bring him a fresh double espresso and one for his colleague. 'I wanted to try and get a sample of his DNA, legally if possible as an illegal procurement would be inadmissible in court. However, for the moment I don't think there is anything more we can do detective sergeant except pass the file on Ella's murder to the public prosecutor and let him decide.'

Chilabon sitting the other side of Bruno's desk, sipped her espresso thoughtfully, unable to offer a viable way forward.

'I would also love to know the extent of Signor Celestini's contributions to Christian Liberal Party funds,' Bruno said with a bitter smile as he put his coffee cup down on the table.

*

Now, the Comune English language lessons had been terminated, Ronnie didn't see as much of his student friends though Mauro had kept in touch with him and had invited him visit the Moro River Canadian War Cemetery, about ten miles up the Adriatic coast near Ortona.

Picking Ronnie up that morning in Mauro's small Italian car outside his apartment, the two of them set off down the hill out of Chieti towards Chieti Scalo and the highway north, skirting Pescara to the east. Mauro, living partly off his parents knew all about living on a budget so commiserated with Ronnie for his, temporarily to be hoped, reduced earnings.

He also had to commiserate with Ronnie for not hearing from Anna ('Is she your girlfriend?' Not exactly,') for a week or so.

Mauro, similarly, under orders to find a suitable girl,

216

preferably church-going, to produce grand children could offer no suitable advice. He had quietly given up trying to find any female interested in World War Two war gaming (always a vain hope) and wondered what other things he may have to compromise in his quest for marital harmony?

His car sped along the bright sunny road on an albeit frosty morning as Ronnie just enjoyed doing something different with a like-minded soul.

*

The walk around the neat expansive cemetery was a sobering experience; so many young men cut down in their prime of lives, hailing from places thousands of miles away, in a determination to set Abruzzo and Italy free from oppression.

The war graves commission, whose information panels fronted the extensive car park, kept the site tidy and respectful with a small white Greek temple style chapel in the middle where visitors could sit and pray and ponder the peaceful surroundings.

An avid Napoleonic war gamer himself, Ronnie felt guilty in some ways for his table top soldering when the young Canadians lying here had soldiered for real and suffered the all too real consequences.

Mauro had told him he was a fascist in reality hadn't he? Did he mean it? Was he sad that Italy had lost the war?

Ronnie decided on reflection, not to delve into his friend's political beliefs at this point beyond sadly concluding he didn't know anyone here in reality. After some perambulations with him around the site and quiet contemplation in the chapel they decided as winter weather was closing in, to call it a day. It was late afternoon and repairing to a wayside restaurant on the way home for a homemade pizza seemed just the trick to round off the day. Later in early evening, Mauro dropped Ronnie at his flat on his way back to Citta Sant' Angelo.

*

Eight p.m.

Later that evening, Ronnie was sitting at his desk in his little apartment and doing some calculations.

It was clear that he could no longer continue the peripatetic English teaching Darius had set up for him. By the end of the month he would be earning the minimum salary which was about fifty per cent down on what he expected.

He would have to call Darius and tell him.

Just then his phone went.

It was Anna.

He couldn't help feeling a pang of satisfaction that she had called *him* first and not the other way round. However, the unhappiness in her voice was clear from the outset, completely disarmed him of any smugness on his part.

This wasn't going to be a conversation he realised, more of a listening exercise.

'The police just rang my uncle. They said they weren't pressing any charges towards Darius Celestini as there was insufficient evidence he had committed any crime. Also Darius was entitled to sack him as he had committed criminal damage in one of Celestini's properties,' she said sadly.

Ronnie could do nothing but side with the authorities. Where was the evidence Darius had been aware of two bodies buried in the grounds of his palazzo? The fact that the bodies has been there for so long suggested he was innocent of their presence.

Ronnie was also aware of Darius being a suspect in the murder of the Comune secretary but was at a loss to understand why he would want to do such a thing?

'What does your uncle want to do then?'

'Well he's angry with Signor Celestini because he reckons Celestini knew about his aunt being buried there. Also...' she hesitated, sighing repeatedly.

'What?' Ronnie pressed her.

'The university are considering asking me to leave my course,' she said sighing again. 'We reckon Signor Celestini rang them and told them I had stolen items from his 'residence' without telling them it was my uncle who had taken his late aunt's possession from inside a recess in a ceiling in one of his apartments. I think Signor Celestini knows people at the university.'

'He can't tell them to do that?' Ronnie replied.

'He can, it seems and has done. My parents and uncle Tomaso are angry and are going to appeal to the university chancellor,' she finished up.

'I am sorry to hear that,' Ronnie found himself repeating himself yet again.

He paused then, 'I am at home now so come round if you like?'

'Okay, Ronnie,' she responded quietly.

'Let's take our minds off the bad things around us,' he tried to sound reassuring but wasn't sure whether the scratchy quality of the line allowed him. 'Stay over if you like instead of going back to your student room so late,' he threw it out there, seeing where it landed.

'Okay, Ron,' she replied again. 'I'll get a taxi so see you in about an hour or so.'

*

It was a telephone conversation Inspector Bruno wasn't relishing.

'Signor Frantoni,' Bruno asked when the phone was answered.

'Yes?'

'This is Inspector Bruno from Chieti Police. Sorry it is Sunday evening but I am calling to give you an update on our investigation into your sister's murder.'

That was the easy bit.

Now the difficult bit.

He had to tell Cesare that the police didn't have enough information to charge anyone with his sister's murder. They had circumstantial evidence but nothing that would lead to a conviction. The public prosecutor would decide the next steps.

Silence at the other end.

Where was the shouting? The recriminations?

'I see,' was all Cesare replied, so quietly that Bruno asked him to speak up, being somewhat disarmed by this behaviour.

This wasn't a normal reaction to the kind of news he had just delivered.

Thursday 8 March – 7.05 a.m.

A misty, rainy morning.

Ronnie was awoken from a deep sleep by his mobile phone ringing by his bed.

He was immediately awake and mobile but he couldn't help waking up Anna, sleeping next to him.

'Mr Cabot?' the smooth accented English voice enquired down the phone. 'Sorry, it's a bit early…'

(Ronnie glanced at his Swatch on the little table next to his bed. Eight o'clock in the morning precisely).

'…but I thought I would get your reaction as soon as,' Darius continued in a business-like manner.

Anna was now awake, yawning and listening intently to the conversation, not least because this was the person angling to be her nemesis? What would he say if he knew she was also there in the bedroom?

She sat up next to Ronnie with her head on his left shoulder, while Ronnie attempted to keep his business-like tone.

'I am transferring you, if you agree Mr Cabot, to Pescara full-time from 1 April to teach English at the university.'

Silence.

'My contact, Signor Gallorio, head of the foreign languages faculty will offer you full-time work and free accommodation near the university, starting 1 September. What do you think?'

'Well…' Ronnie started. 'Sounds good but I want to see a contract Mr Celestini.'

'Of course. I am coming round in a while to take you to see my contact at the university and your flat, if that's okay with you?'

'Well, Mr Celestini,' Ronnie replied, pulling his knees up in bed covered by his duvet and Anna resting on his back behind him. 'It's a lot of information you're giving me so early in the morning.'

A pause.

'Okay then, I'll have a look at what Signor Gallorio is offering. Give an hour to get up and have breakfast then okay?'

'I'll be outside at ten thirty then, bye.'

With that he was gone.

Ronnie and Anna were left in some shock at the sudden turn of events and struggled to evaluate what they had heard.

The realisation that both needed to get on gripped them as they both hopped out of bed in a rush without even being able to think about their first night spent together, though the smiles round both of their lips betrayed a sensation of joyous exhilaration carried along by new love and a renewed readiness to face Satan and all his legions, foreign and domestic.

*

The man's puckered lips betrayed a seething indignation as he parked his car in a Chieti side street, just along the road from the Comune.

He was supposed to be at work at his prestigious architectural practice meeting clients and working on orders but he couldn't work.

He couldn't focus on anything since the murder of his sister.

His family had been devastated.

However, the mood had slowly changed to outrage when they had found out her boyfriend was a copper. He had done nothing to bring her killer to justice! No one had been charged and his sister's death was just another attachment stored on a computer and consigned to oblivion.

He walked along the street, eyes down at the pavement – unusual for the time of day when most others were going briskly to work in the cold morning rain. He looked like he was going home at the end of a long day, not starting one.

The sharp bladed instrument was concealed in the tatty white plastic bag.

A bit conspicuous, if truth be told, but on a winter's morning when commuters were going to work, no one lingered long enough to pick the man up for it.

He arrived at the police station and hovered at the entrance, unsure of his next move.

A couple of visitors entered through the revolving doors creating a brief swoosh of air wafted in his general direction.

He was in a limbo.

How would he find his quarry?

It was a large sprawling brick building, covered in CCTV he noticed, even as he looked up and down the street in the cold morning air.

He had been noticed.

Station Sergeant Degrelli, always with one eye on the station entrance while he was on duty, soon spotted the loiterer and made his way over to the entrance.

The loiterer started to panic. If this big, uniformed man got in his way, how on earth was he to get in? How could he…

'Hey you!' Degrelli shouted. 'What do you want? You can't wait there!' he said advancing on the stranger who started away from the main entrance before breaking into a run down the pavement, not stopping to look back.

The police sergeant was never going to give chase, but not having got a look at the man, decided that the incident was over and slowly pushed the revolving door forward so he could go back into the station and out of the cold.

*

Cesare Frantoni was even more disturbed, having been thwarted in one plan he had, decided there was always a plan B.

He had already managed to get in the Comune car park because the security was so lax. The two guards were either in the Comune *ristorante* having refreshment, completely against the rules which said only one at a time could do so, or just not on duty full stop. He knew whereabouts the employees cars were parked in their reserved spaces so all he had to do was to hide round the back of the car and wait.

*

Five p.m.

The fingerprint results from the security camera in the Comune basement popped onto Dom Drago's laptop from the forensics department.

The inspector sat up in his chair as he took in the momentous news.

Orazio Mancetti's prints were all over it.

'Amanda!' Drago shouted through his office door. 'Let's get over to the Comune right away! Mancetti has some questions to answer!'

*

Cesare Frantoni awoke with a start, crouched round the back of the Ford Focus as the car's driver's side door opened.

He desperately needed to pee but there was nowhere nearby which added to his frenzied behaviour.

His quarry, the man he had been waiting for, had got into the driver's seat and was about to slam the door closed.

Quick as a flash, the waiting man rushed round to the driver's side and wedged his body between the door and the car frame, shouting his lungs out.

'What the hell...?' Orazio Mancetti managed to say as he tried to eject the attacker from his driver's door frame and close it.

'You killed my sister you bastard. Fucking rot in hell,' he shouted as he pulled the kitchen knife out of the manky plastic bag and stabbed the driver in the chest.

The driver, mortally wounded, screaming and flailing his arms as he seemed to punch the attacker with his right hand as he tried to slide out of the car.

The attacker, shouting at his victim, filling the atmosphere around them with oaths and curses, held on to the knife as both attacker and victim fell out of the car and onto the concrete floor.

There was blood everywhere as the driver, gradually losing energy began to be still while his attacker, somehow badly wounded himself, attempted to retrieve the knife and do more damage.

Before the attacker could do more, two white-shirted men grabbed him from behind, attempting to grab the now free knife

225

before the attacker could use it on them.

Soon, all four were on the cold concrete floor with each of the security men holding one coat arm of the attacker.

By now their shirts were covered in blood and dirt as the attacker's was.

Like his victim, the assailant had also gone limp.

Frantic cries for an ambulance were shouted to colleagues slowly arriving to help subdue the attacker and provide first aid for the victim.

The latter, identified as Signor Orazio Mancetti, the principal secretary for the Christian Liberal Party, was beyond help as he lay spread out on the concrete floor covered in blood. Before he could be taken away he was respectfully covered in a dark blanket, retrieved from the security office until the police could arrive.

The attacker, himself having suffered seemingly unexplained stab wounds himself in his mortal fight with the victim, was sent off to the hospital under armed guard, in the suburbs of Chieti.

The same hospital where Ella had been taken to.

*

5.17 p.m.

Inspector Bruno cursed loudly as he heard on the police radio about a stabbing in Chieti Comune car park – DS Chilabon sitting in the passenger's seat becoming more anxious to get there as soon as possible.

Bruno's police car, siren wailing was still minutes away as he immediately guessed a link between his emergency dash and the simultaneous attack in the municipal basement.

226

Tearing into underground Comune car park by-passing uniformed policemen guarding the entrance, a chaotic, bloody crime scene presented itself.

'Jesus Christ!' Drago blurted out, hearing the officer on duty's interim report on what had transpired barely twenty minutes ago.

'If only we'd got here sooner sir,' Chilabon replied frowning at the bloody crime scene. 'We might have nabbed Frantoni before he could stab Mancetti.'

'It seems sir that no one knew Mancetti himself carried a lock-knife in his driver's door pocket, least of all the attacker Frantoni,' the officer replied, showing Inspector Drago the bloody door pocket, cordoned off by police tape.

'Yeah, seems Frantoni never expected Mancetti to attack *him*, however, serious Mancetti's condition,' Drago responded after glancing at the messy driver's door towards the discarded blood-soaked knife lying on the ground nearby.

The policeman's radio again crackled into life.

Bruno took the phone offered to him, hearing stuttering bursts of dialogue from the police officers at the hospital where Frantoni had been taken.

Bruno's sigh as he lowered his arm holding the phone told all assembled all they needed to know.

'Mancetti and Frantoni both dead on arrival. Both from stab wounds,' Inspector Bruno said, looking up sadly. 'First Ella Frantoni and now her brother.'

'God! Their poor parents,' Amanda replied bitterly, before sitting down briefly on a plastic chair provided by the Comune staff upstairs.

Scene of crime personnel knowing the inspector's personal involvement in the case, went quietly about their business.

'Can you go to Frantoni's office to inform his work-colleagues DS Chilabon? Bruno asked his colleague. Also ask a male and female police officer to go to the Frantoni parents' address please,' Bruno added quietly as he got on his mobile phone to Sergeant Degrelli at police headquarters.

'I called Signora Ceresa sir and then without any prompting told me that Signor Mancetti was involved in passing information on about Ella's activities at the Comune, probably to Celestini, but he should have been prosecuted in a court of law,' Degrelli continued, filling in the inspector on the latest events. 'You want me to bring her in again sir?'

'No Sergeant, no need.'

'You might say he got what he deserved then sir?' Degrelli hazarded.

'Which one of them are you talking about? Bruno replied bitterly.

All he knew was that all this blood stemmed from him losing his beloved Ella and probably *he* was to blame, Bruno concluded.

'I should have told her to get away, go on holiday Filipo. I should have…'

'You can't blame yourself sir,' Degrelli responded, still on the line.

'Can't I?' he asked turning to his friend with his lips tight together. 'Now two other people are dead because of what I asked her to do.'

'Go home sir, I will monitor the investigation for now and clear anything with the powers that be.'

To his surprise perhaps, Bruno got up without argument and with a cursory goodbye his station sergeant at his word and walked slowly up to the car park entrance and into the bustling street outside.

As he walked, he called firstly Deputy Nerone to inform him of the events in the Comune car park and then his colleague

228

Inspector Drago back in his Rome HQ. The significance of Mancetti's fingerprints on the security camera had already leaked out to the press who had a field day writing about local government corruption (again).

'So, the mayor didn't know Mancetti was monitoring who went into the Comune basement then?' Drago asked, his eyebrows as well as his voice moving slowly upwards.

'Apparently not,' Bruno replied. 'He then went on TV to officially deny it. The Liberal Democratic party employees have now been banned from accessing any Comune areas outside their official offices,' Bruno added with a self-conscious smirk. Liberal Democratic HQ in Rome are now involved too!'

'If only Ella's camera had survived enough in a condition for us to retrieve the pictures she took,' Bruno continued. 'But I suspect she had photographed Palazzo Gran Sasso documents that probably have now gone.'

'It's a pity Celestini's dabs weren't on the camera,' Drago continued. 'Surely he put Mancetti up to it with Mancetti's palm suitable greased. What's your plan to reel him in then Jordi?'

'He's a slippery bastard Dom but he won't escape sure as eggs are definitely eggs!'

*

9.55 p.m.
Jordi Bruno sat up late nursing a large whiskey as he gazed out of his window towards the sea.

Amanda had called him to update him on her sad visit to Frantoni's former work place and the outcome of the police visit to the Frantoni residence.

She was of course, as much interested in how her boss was coping as much as passing on latest developments.

Jordi was touched by her concern while her family life

played out in the background.

*

Alone with his thoughts in the darkened room lit just by a study lamp on the desk opposite, he relentlessly bit his lip as he questioned his judgment on using his civilian girlfriend to covertly gather information from the Comune basement.

She *had* acquiesced to his wishes and taken risks though Bruno thought in event of her being found out she would be only sacked.

He had never expected she would lose her life as a result. Someone must have been frantic that their secret dealings remained just that even if it had meant murder.

He fixed himself another large Bowmore whisky, his favourite, with an ice-cube to tickle it a bit.

Was that her sitting opposite? he considered. Smiling at him?

He stopped and stared.

Beyond him and outside the far window the dark waters of the Adriatic pounded onto a distant sandy shore.

'I'm so sorry Ella,' Jordi Bruno called out. 'My love, my life.'

The silence around him cried out for a response.

Instead in Bruno's head there was her comforting voice. 'Don't worry Jordi. I am at peace now. All my love.'

Beyond the front window, life went on.

Cars drove past as well as the occasional pedestrian with or without a pet to walk.

Jordi Bruno resolved himself to focus on the present and leave the past to look after the past.

Friday 16 March – p.m.

It was Ronnie's first night in his new first floor apartment in a low-rise apartment block, a mile or so from his office in the University of Pescara's foreign languages faculty.

A comfortable residence with two bedrooms, a living room, bathroom and small kitchen, it overlooked the main road into town rather than Roman ruins in a picturesque little square he had previously enjoyed.

Sitting on the narrow balcony and looking out at the starry sky he reminded himself of the fascination he had had for Edward Hopper's painting *'Nighthawks at the diner,'* which had hung in his best friend's house in Reading back home in England.

Ronnie and his friend had always pondered who *they* were in the painting? Was Ronnie indeed, the man with the girlfriend?

Or was she a mistress having a nightcap with her lover in a bar slowly winding down?

Or maybe she was a prostitute which explained her unrestrained joy at the prospect of a big pay out from her new client?

Ronnie was probably the lone male figure in the corner of the bar or even the cheery barman but wouldn't admit it. He was a teacher not a barman.

Now, growing closer to Anna, perhaps he was now the man with the girl at the bar who was in fact his girlfriend? Now he was sharing intimacies with someone similar in real life so had life now started to imitate art?

*

Anna then arrived at his apartment in a smart white shirt and jeans and joined him at the little wooden table on the balcony.

Looking in Ronnie's eyes, she was for him a picture of beauty.

Then he realised.

He had indeed always known her.

'Have you heard of Edward Hopper?

'No who's he? An actor? She asked smiling.

'No, he painted a picture called *Nighthawks* and you are in it,' he replied also smiling.

Anna beamed back, holding his hand tightly, sitting next to him on the balcony.

'I'll show it you online. Then you'll will realise we are both constructionists by the way!' Ronnie said laughing which caused her to chuckle away. 'I did my homework darling!'

Her university student room was within walking distance of Ronnie's flat. Indeed, some of his new English classes were to be in the same building where she had her lectures.

She had ordered by phone, kebabs with salad while Ronnie had just got two cold Nastroni beers from the fridge.

He broached the subject of her uncle.

Immediately a cloud passed in front of her, making Ronnie sigh that he had brought up the subject in the first place.

'He has no job. He says he has been blacklisted by employers in Chieti,' she said picking at her kebab.

'Has he, do you think?'

'We can't tell,' she replied but everyone knows how much influence Signor Celestini has in the area. Who's to disagree?'

Ronnie felt sorry for Anna and her family but moved the subject entirely off Daruis Celestini's influence on their lives.

'What about your place at the university?' he asked.

'I appealed against their decision and I have still to hear,' she replied.

'Let's hope it's a positive decision them,' he smiled back at her.

*

Even, when they later sat arm in arm watching TV later on in the evening, Ronnie's past life as Celestini's employee hadn't disappeared entirely.

The inquests had opened on Orazio Mancetti and Cesare Frantoni, the TV reporter announced from outside Chieti's Coroner's Court.

'He was your student right?' Anna said looking at him.

'Yes,' Ronnie sighed, sitting up and putting his beer down. 'What's the reporter saying?' he asked the translator sitting next to him.

'He's talking about the violent confrontation in the car park between the Christian Liberal Party Secretary who was getting into his car and a man whose sister had been murdered a month previously. This man blamed the party secretary for the murder and was incensed when he heard that the police didn't have enough evidence to charge anyone in connection. The brother took matters into his own hands to revenge himself but never realised that the party secretary too had a knife in his car and the attack resulted in both of their deaths.'

'God,' Ronnie responded, sitting back in his chair. 'I knew Orazaio Mancetti as the life and soul of my English lessons at the

Comune. I never would have thought he would have been involved in a murder.'

'This is small town Italy dear,' Anna replied in her gently accentuated English. 'You can see how everyone knows everyone. Italians are friendly on the surface but like you found out in your apartment at the palazzo, secrets from our painful past are still around and being exposed. Some people don't want that, including people you know and I know.'

Finding refuge in each other that night seemed the best medicine they knew to restore a little bit of happiness for them both.

Monday 19 March – 2.02 p.m.

Ronnie Cabot was walking down the main road in Chieti Scalo having just got off the bus from Pescara, on his way to his remaining English lessons with the medical students he had already inherited from Darius. As their medical training centre also served as their classroom, they were unaffected when Darius Celestini closed down his own Language centre. He had heard that Tiziana had found work in another company in Pescara where she lived so commuting was a lot shorter though her work now might not be as light.

Ronnie was about to cross the road when he heard someone shouting to him from a car parked up on the side.

It was his former student Mauro and someone else sitting in a smart BMW.

He went over and greeted his friend, grateful to catch up after not seeing each other for a while.

Ronnie told Mauro about his new job at the university in Pescara with one class left in Chieti Scalo while Mauro told him about starting his own business as a Graphic Designer.

'This is Vincenzo Mancetti,' Mauro said indicating the driver next to him.

Ronnie smiled as honestly as he could.

It seemed Vincenzo did the same.

'Sorry about what happened to your brother,' Ronnie offered.

Vincenzo, dressed casually, albeit in designer clobber from

head to foot kept his sunglasses on and pointedly failed to say anything again, in Italian or English beyond a cursory nod.

An awkward conversation continued, not because Ronnie wasn't happy to see Mauro but wondered how Orazio's brother had evaluated Ronnie's role in the tragic events.

Ronnie Cabot hadn't done anything wrong.

Was he guilty therefore by association?

After inviting Mauro to visit him in his new flat, he decided he had to go so waving the pair in the car off, he headed across the road to the Medical Centre for his English lesson.

*

Ronnie had also decided not to talk about Anna and their new relationship with anyone for now.

It didn't seem really appropriate given that she was the niece of the car park attendant/maintenance man sacked by Darius.

Would Orazio or Mauro think he, Ronnie was just some arrogant foreigner coming in and grabbing some nice local girl? Did they think he had contributed to the mystery in some way? Why hadn't he just put up with a cold apartment and liberally used the fan heater? Celestini had been paying his utility bills after all?

Cabot decided to stop worrying and go to work.

In spite of the sad events at the Comune and the two murders, three if you counted the murderer Frantoni, Ronnie decided he had to get on with his life and not get stuck on what happened or what might have been?

He had a new job, nice flat and nice girlfriend so that was what he wanted to concentrate on.

Wednesday 21 March – Eight a.m.

The news report on TV said that the Regional Public Prosecutor had decided there was insufficient evidence for charges to be brought against local businessman Darius Celestini over two bodies found buried in his property, namely the Palazzo Gran Sasso.

As a result, a disgruntled ex-employee noisily put his espresso down in disgust, almost spilling the dregs on the printed cotton table cloth of his little apartment kitchen.

He then walked out of the apartment building in a Chieti suburb and took a bus up to the Corso Marrucino, getting off mid-way along its busy thoroughfare.

Witnesses would later tell the police the man seemed almost as if he were in a trance.

Wearing his flat cap and a battered raincoat, clearly inadequate against the inclement weather, he trudged down the Corso in Chieti town centre. People in one's and two's huddled past him in every direction as they tried to spend as little time as possible outside.

Presently, he arrived at his destination, a large early 20th century baroque-style palazzo where if one stopped long enough, one could still hear the sounds of children behind large thick-plated windows.

He pushed open the heavy wooden doors and the inside glass revolving versions, and walked past the reception area where it seemed there was no one to challenge him – perhaps he had been a familiar character there previously.

He then plodded up the central marble staircase already half an eye on the office he was aiming for. Children laughing, talking, mixed in with adult voices were all around him though strangely none of them could be seen.

He arrived at the door of the office he was looking for and looked in.

There was the man he was after, on the phone as usual, dressed in one of his designer suits sitting behind his cluttered desk with two other mobile phones on it.

The visitor stood at the threshold and waited for the man to look up.

'What do you want?' the man behind the desk asked in a surly voice seeing his unwelcome guest hovering on the threshold.

'Justice,' the visitor said quietly.

'Get out before I call the cops,' the man snorted. 'How did you get in past reception? How…?'

Before he could ask his third question, the visitor pulled open his raincoat and took out a vintage luger pistol, with which he pumped several bullets into the seated victim.

Before the figures outside running and shouting in the corridor could arrive on the scene, Signor Tomaso Scilaci pumped the last bullet into his own head as his former employer Darius Celestini lay sprawled in a bloody heap behind his desk and messing up the luxury beige curtain beside him.

*

Soon afterwards, in the mayhem of children being rushed out of the building with teachers and paramedics attempting to find order in chaos, two figures slowly made their way downstairs. Their nonchalant behaviour jarred noticeably with the panicky people all around them.

They seemed happy, even smiling as they walked down the marble stairs arm in arm to the entrance of the building.

Why were they never once challenged?

Tomaso Scilaci was dressed in an old raincoat and Margaretta Embriaco was dressed in an old-fashioned khaki uniform.

Simple.

They were invisible.

Thursday 22 March – Eight Fifteen a.m.

The world of English language teaching in Chieti and its environs was in shock.

Ronnie, being about to meet his Thursday morning grammar class for the first time when Bernie rang him frantically.

The news was unbelievable.

Ronnie weakened and sat down on the floor against the wall as his legs gave way.

Darius Celestini shot dead in his office by Tomaso Scilaci who then shot himself!

In the middle of a busy school day!

Ronnie didn't cry though.

Darius wasn't family but he was shocked at the genial palazzo's maintenance man could have done such a thing.

Bernie didn't know what would happen to the school but all the teachers and students had been sent home for the rest of the week.

Would it open on the following Monday?

Ronnie Cabot took several deep breaths as he got up and went into an empty classroom and sat on an empty chair, his arms hung down like useless implements.

Had Darius been hiding his history?

Known about the bodies in the palazzo?

Whatever the answers he hadn't deserved his terrible end surely?

It was the second brutal murder in broad daylight of

someone connected to Ronnie.

He had to go to his class, so sighing and with a hang dog expression, he put his best foot forward and went to meet his class.

Early June

Darius Celestini's murder had consequences for Chieti in general and the police department in particular.

The language school never re-opened after his murder.

The lawyers, executors of his estate, laid off all the staff and the students' courses were terminated, forcing those who wanted to learn the most significant world language to seek tuition elsewhere; Pescara for example.

The papers reported on Signor Celestini's tangled tax affairs as well as murky property and business dealings, leaving those who knew him or worked for him, alternately shocked, saddened and angry. Particularly, when Signor Celestini was named as the alleged suspect in the murder of Ella Frantoni. The motive the police considered was that Frantoni had found documents in the Comune archives that proved Celestini's father – presumed dead – had fraudulently acquired the Palazzo Gran Sasso by means unknown at the present time and therefore Darius Celestini's ownership of said palazzo was open to question.

The degree to which he ran his little empire with such determination, even to killing to keep it, caused those who read about him to shake their heads in disbelief.

Ronnie Cabot, while not being a close friend of the late businessman could only tell Anna that Darius had always looked after him as an employee and the picture the police painted of him was almost another man.

A few days later, there appeared at Chieti police station from the USA a recorded delivery letter. The name on the return slip address was Angelo Celestini.

So Darius had had a son.

This was news!

Inspector Jordi Bruno was sitting in his office reading and rereading the letter Celestini had written.

Something in his brain had been activated by his return to the events surrounding the discovery of the body in Palazzo Gran Sasso.

It was something the teacher Ronnie had told him the Contessa had said, *'I know you don't have to go far to solve the mystery.'*

Bruno sat and thought.

His colleague Inspector Domenico Drago had had to go into the Apennine mountains to supposedly solve the mystery of Major Molina's whereabouts.

Under the black granite slab with only old Vasco and his son Ennio in charge of everything.

What was the snippet of speech Darius had used about his father *using the present tense*?

Why would Celestini have spoken about him like that unless he knew something the police didn't?

'Old Vasco,' Bruno slowly said aloud to the door opposite.

'Old Vasco my arse!'

Jordi Bruno was out of his chair as though he had been riding a rocket.

'Amanda!' he shouted across the reception area to the collection of desks where several Carabinieri were working on computers. 'Organise a couple of cars to wait outside and some uniforms to fill them! We're paying *old Vasco* another visit! Oh and bring some shovels!'

'Who sir?' DS Chilabon was momentarily stumped by this name her boss waved under her nose from some corner of his mind.

Bruno was too busy to engage with his detective sergeant.

He turned to Sergeant Degrelli, 'Find me the route Inspector Drago took when he went to Celestini's farm above the Alterno-Pescara river in March okay? Then get a uniform to programme into the sat-nav on the lead car we are using from the car pool. I want to go now!'

Sergeant Degrelli nodded and picked up his phone to track down the sat-nav the previous inspector had used.

*

A couple of hours later, Inspector Bruno accompanied by several Carabinieri arrived in the flashing blue Alfa Romeo police car convoy at the site at the remote farm in the Apennine foothills where Darius Celestini had indicated his father lay buried.

There was the gate.

Duly opened again by the younger man with the older man there again in the bright conservatory.

The two police cars pulled up on the verge and everyone got out.

The bewildered elderly man sat still with his arms in his lap as he was approached then carefully apprehended.

Putting an elderly man into the back of the second car was an achievement in itself as the police Alfa Romeo then turned around and gingerly made its way back down the track to the main road – DS Chilabon accompanying the suspect back to police HQ.

The other Alfa Romeo proceeded to the farm yard where Inspector Bruno, and two other policemen, Castello and Carboni walked over in clear sunny weather to the little orchard and the black granite grave marker.

The granite marker proved to be tightly wedged into the ground Only the combined efforts of three policemen and their shovels that the marker was finally lifted from the hard earth .

All three officers peered into the hole.

A dirty wooden box with black metal clasps sat several feet down.

Three pairs of eyes peered down with the same 'sinking' feeling.

'We can't get it out,' Bruno informed the little congregation. 'But we're not giving up.'

*

Inspector Bruno couldn't wait to bring his colleague Domenico Drago up to speed with events of the day.

'Yes it all makes sense when you think about it,' Drago said finally as his friend brought him up to speed. 'Hiding in plain sight, I suppose you call it?'

'Molina as he admitted his name easily enough, is now in our police cell,' Bruno informed his colleague, but considering his age, I'm not sure the courts will want to do much in the way of prosecuting him. We are still investigating his carer but any charges there seem a bit flimsy.'

'Did Molina know about his son's murder?'

'To be honest I'm not sure,' Bruno responded. 'I might get

245

more out of him when Celestini's son arrives in Chieti from the US. The buried box with the gold bars was definitely a surprise. We have impounded it and are investigating the numbers carved on their sides. There are no reports of recent gold thefts so I think they date back a long time, maybe to war-time and wherever Molina got them, they may have been the source of Celestini's fortune,' he finished up.

Jordi Bruno had one more task to perform.

He chased up the pathology lab in Pescara.

*

Ronnie was on his afternoon coffee break from teaching Intermediate English at the university foreign languages when he got an excited message from Anna who had started a summer waitressing job in a busy down town restaurant.

'The university are letting me stay at the university! I can resume my course in October!'

'So glad for you,' Ronnie texted back.

Obviously, the fallout from Darius Celestini's murder had resulted in Anna Bianca being taken off the list of unsuitable candidates to study, now the main mover against her was dead.

Though Darius had been his employer, Ronnie thought he had gone too far and that she should be reinstated.

*

Late June – 11.10 a.m.
It was the day before Ronnie would travel back to the UK by train to work in an EFL summer school as a teacher. His Pescara teaching job would restart in October.

He and Anna sat on the seafront at Francavilla, a few miles from inland Chieti. In front of them large numbers of sunbathers lounged on towels and swimmers splashed and called in calm Adriatic sea.

They young couple sat on a wooden bench eating ice creams, under a warm blue sunny sky.

Ronnie scanned the English newspaper he had bought in Pescara that morning and started laughing.

'What?' Anna asked, holding her melting cornet and turning away from the sea to look at him.

'It says here, *"Plans to close the local Cemetery in Brentwood have been put on hold until interested bodies have been consulted."*'

She looked blank.

'In English a body means a person but also an organisation,' he said starting to laugh.

A kind of smile appeared on Anna's lips as she tried to join in, not really appreciating English humour.

'Honestly darling, it is funny!' he said putting his arm round her shoulder.

'If you say so.'

*

'Of course, I'll miss you,' he said later, reassuring her anxious expression as she sat close to him as they watched the waves coming in. 'I'll be back in two months don't worry,' he finished up smiling into her pinched pale face. She had to hear these words he realised. She couldn't just assume it apparently.

He didn't want to ask her about her family since her uncle had committed suicide. It was a big family anyway so he thought

247

his comments were not necessary. He surmised that Anna would be well taken care of.

*

Inspector Bruno sat at his desk as the emails he had been waiting for pinged up on the screen.

Metaphorically rolling his sleeves up, he prepared to open the email and perhaps confirm what he had long suspected.

He slowly read the first one, in English as it happened, as he had wanted a second opinion with his opposite number in the Metropolitan Police in London.

He then sat back and called in his in-house waiter for a double espresso.

Detective Sergeant Chilabon walked into his office, without knocking he mentally noted. Something's rattled her, he thought knowingly. Her eyebrows were on the ceiling!

'Sir,' she said breathlessly, 'sorry about just walking in but have you seen the email that says...'

'Yes, yes, finally,' Jordi Bruno said holding up his right hand to indicate please stop right there.

He motioned for her to sit down.

The waiter knocked and came in with Bruno's double espresso.

Bruno asked him to return with another one for Amanda.

'It is as we thought Amanda all along, though perhaps in the backs of our minds.'

'The DNA test confirmed my suspicions anyway,' she said. 'Signor Celestini's fingerprint was on the taxi driver's banknote. He deliberately drove that poor girl off the road.'

Jordi Bruno drank his coffee and sighed audibly.

He almost said a prayer for the soul of Ella Frantoni there and then, but held back. This should be a private response rather than a public one from him. He vowed to light a candle though for her next time he was going past the cathedral.

'Not only was the late Signor Celestini a murderer but his mother had lived in a poky little apartment walled off from the original apartment which it had been part of. I can't understand why neither of them acknowledged the other?' Chilabon continued, eyes widening as she sat and sighed in Bruno's leather chair in front of his desk.

'Yes, it bothers me too,' he replied with genuine sadness. 'I asked my opposite number in London at the Metropolitan police for a second opinion on the DNA sample we retrieved from the Contessa's body. They duly concurred with our suspicions. None of it explains why they lived their lives ignoring each other,' Jordi Bruno continued shaking his head. 'We couldn't lock Celestini up for anything before the murder. We just spooked him by letting him think we could!'

'I don't think she was even a real Contessa either sir. I couldn't find any other family members with such a name.'

'Probably she used it as an affectation,' Bruno said sadly. 'God knows why?'

'What about the gold bars?' Chilabon asked.

'I don't know – maybe we could have charged him with handling stolen gold? Maybe he would have been sunk with a massive tax bill? He wouldn't have lost everything I am certain. A man like him with his connections? Now, we know Celestini had a son, maybe that changes everything? We shall see how much of an estate the young man inherits.'

Head shaking and lip biting had become infectious as both officers indulged.

They sipped their espressos in silence as they continued to read the pathologist's findings.

'It's strange though sir,' Amanda said, finishing her espresso. 'None of this would have come to light if Signor Celestini had maintained his property a bit better? Fancy that! A cold apartment for the English teacher Mr Cabot resulted in, how many murders?' she asked, sighing.

*

In a side street in a quiet Roman suburb, National Party Secretary for the Christian Liberal Party Lettieri sat in a parked car with two other men.

'We called you here Signor Lettieri,' the man said, 'because the Chieti police found the gold bars hidden at Celestini's farm. He sold them to us. Now they are gone. We want compensation.'

'Your gold bars?' Lettieri hissed angrily. 'Is that all you care about? They belong to the party now. Our contact in Chieti Signor Mancetti's was brutally murdered – only mitigated by the fact that he took the bastard who killed him Frantoni with him,' he added bitterly. 'Mancetti was just protecting an important local member Signor Celestini who was himself gunned down in his school as you saw in the media.'

'We helped you suppress your party man Celestini's fingerprints and his car details so the police came to a dead end. Are you saying Signor you are of no use to us any more?' the man asked casually.

'Listen,' Lettieri was getting exasperated. 'We could make sure the party gains control of Signor Celestini's properties and assets. The old Nazi father is too isolated as far as I know and too old to protest,' his companion offered. We just need another man

250

in charge of the party we can rely on. No outsider to rock the boat,' the Secretary continued.

His two companions had heard enough and were not convinced by this yesterday's man.

Silently and in the blink of an eye, the man sitting behind the National Party Secretary pulled out a small snub-nosed gun and silencer and shot Lettieri in the back of the head.

The secretary lurched forward, hitting his head on the front windscreen in a bloody heap before slumping down on the passenger seat.

The two men wearing gloves and dark glasses exited the car and walked off down the street.

When they reached the crossroads and headed towards The massive ruins of the Baths of Caracalla, they casually put back their small police badges back on the lapels of their coats and switched back on their official phones.

*

Last day of June – 9.05 a.m.

'Ciao chietino,' Anna said as Ronnie put his suitcase and bags onto the intercity express bound for Paris and onwards to the English Channel.

He smiled back at her as he held her on the platform.

'Did you hear about the two Englishman who lived on a desert island but never spoke to each other?' Ronnie asked as he gently flicked back a curl of her black hair.

'No,' she replied with a tear in one eye. 'What about them?'

'Do you know why they never spoke?'

'Why?' she asked.

'They hadn't been introduced,' Ronnie replied with a smile.

Anna struggled to smile, trying to understand the English humour.

Ronnie laughed out loud, causing train travellers either side to turn and look at them.

'Don't worry I'll be back soon,' he continued leaving the joke behind. 'I'll call you when I am at summer school, okay?'

She sighed and shed another tear as the stationmaster (not Bernardo on this occasion) blew his whistle.

Kissing her one more time, Ronnie Cabot climbed back into the railway carriage and waved from the main door.

The train slowly pulled out as Anna stood on the platform waving and sighing as she puckered her lips together to suppress a sob.

She sadly made her way back to her university study room but not before making a quick detour to the Pharmacy.

In the privacy of her en suite bathroom she performed a small test to confirm what she had already suspected.

The result was positive...